A Cupcake Christmas

A Christmas Elf Romance

Touchstone Series, #5

By Beth Barany

Other Books by Beth Barany

Touchstone Series, Romance Novellas, Books 1-4
Touchstone of Love
A Christmas Fling
Parisian Amour
A Labyrinth of Love and Roses

The Five Kingdom Series
Henrietta The Dragon Slayer, Book 1
Henrietta and the Dragon Stone, Book 2

Barany School of Fiction Books for Writers
Overcome Writer's Block
The Writer's Adventure Guide
Twitter for Authors

A Cupcake Christmas

A Christmas Elf Story

Touchstone Series #5

Beth Barany

Firewolf Books

OAKLAND, CALIFORNIA

A CUPCAKE CHRISTMAS, A CHRISTMAS ELF STORY, TOUCHSTONE SERIES #5

Copyright © 2015 by Beth Barany

Firewolf Books
771 Kingston Ave., #108
Piedmont, California, 94611
www.firewolfbooks.com

Publisher's Note: This is a work of fiction. Names, characters, places, and incidents are a product of the author's imagination. Locales and public names are sometimes used for atmospheric purposes. Any resemblance to actual people, living or dead, or to businesses, companies, events, institutions, or locales is completely coincidental.

Book Layout ©2015 BookDesignTemplates.com
Book Design by Beth Barany
Cover Design by Beth & Ezra Barany
Cover Art by Beth Barany

Quantity sales. Special discounts are available on quantity purchases by corporations, associations and others. For details, contact the "Special Sales Department" at the address above.

A Cupcake Christmas A Christmas Elf Story, Touchstone Series #5/
Beth Barany. -- 1st ed.
ISBN: 978-0-9895004-7-0 (ISBN 10: 0989500470)

To the magic of love. May you cook up some for yourself!

Chapter One

"Help wanted. Must be good with pastry baking, parties + kids. Part-time/Holiday temporary. Competitive pay. Flexible hours. Apply in person. Bring printed resume. Must love cupcakes."

Florian jumped off the trolley at the bottom of Market Street and checked the address on his smart phone's map. He peered around at the busy area, looking for his new possible employment, Kate's Cupcake Cart. He didn't see it. He must be off by a few blocks. He hustled back up Market Street, one of San Francisco's main boulevards.

A cold brisk wind had him turning up his collar, pulling down his cap more over his ears—couldn't have people spotting them and asking questions—and tightening his scarf. He loved the weather at the city on the bay. Way warmer than New York City where he'd been working up to last week, and way, way warmer than back home at the Pole.

He stood on the busy street corner of the city's Financial District and swiveled, not just his head, but his whole body. He still didn't see it. He was about to wave his hand to stir up some magic, maybe bring a magnifying glass in front of him—he never knew exactly what he'd conjure—but then saw as the busy crowd thinned for a moment what he was looking for. A small food stand perched on the corner, kitty corner to where he stood. A big sprinkle-top cupcake jauntily capped the sign that stated in broad flourish font, "Kate's Cupcake Cart." At the other end of the sign, a frothy cappuccino angled in nice symmetry. He smiled. His sign-making elf cousins couldn't have done a better job.

He crossed the street, a bounce in his step, and wiggled his fingers in his pockets. Nerves. This job would work out. Had to. He needed one more stint of unique work experience to round out his resume, emphasis on the unique. Uncle, known as Santa to the rest of the world, expected him to have a diverse and eclectic resume when he returned home to finally ascend to his rightful place as Master Baker for the entire North Pole community. He was young for a Master Baker but ambitious. He still had to prove himself.

He approached the cupcake cart and stood in line, already ten people deep at 9 a.m. He bounced up and down on his toes. A busy boutique business, how fun. What a refreshing change from the bigger business he'd worked in recently. He'd mostly worked in storefronts or pastry kitchens this past year. He was almost done with his year abroad. His family would so delight in his travels. He couldn't wait to tell them about his confection adventures at the festivities Christmas morning.

Exciting San Francisco was his last stop. A nice bonus. There was something special about this sparkling city by the bay. Another bonus: He'd enjoy a taste of a mild winter before returning home.

What better way to end his year abroad than to make cupcakes in a vibrant city for quirky Californians? Now he just needed to wow the proprietor of this cute establishment for the final flourish to his resume.

Kate Delore finished making the double cap dry with a flick of her wrist, creating her signature swirl on the foam, and handed it to the salt-and-pepper suit-and-tie customer. On the counter, her cell phone buzzed. In quick succession, the heater oven dinged and her phone buzzed again. She handed the man his warmed chocolate croissant cupcake, zapped his iPhone to transact the payment, and thanked him. He replied in French, and then English, smiled at her, and went on his way. She liked her cosmopolitan customers. Maybe one day she'd be able to buy a croissant in Paris and say thank you in English and French. She didn't have time to dwell on the daydream—when did she ever have time—when her phone buzzed a third time.

She ignored it since at the window the next customer waited. The call was probably another lunch order. She'd have to take it at the next break. She made a mental note to look into an answering service. Kate glanced at the customer, ready to greet him. The tall red-haired man gave her a bright smile. She blinked at him, taken aback by his high-wattage happiness that seemed to roll off him in waves of sunlight.

"A good morning to you," he said with a lilt.

"Good morning. What would you like?" She glanced at the caller ID when the phone buzzed yet again.

Another number she didn't recognize. It could be another lunch order, or someone calling about the help wanted ad, or about booking another birthday party. She made a list in her mind for the tenth time this morning—that answering service, another baker, more customer service help so she could breathe a little, and—why not—a personal masseuse and some time away from the business. May as well throw in those last ones too since she was crafting a wish list.

The man didn't reply to her question, so she glanced back at him.

He was craning his head into her food stand and nodding as if he approved of what he saw.

"Can I help you?" she said, maybe more sharply than she should have to a potential customer. But he was ogling her cart. She checked the time on her phone. Mike would be arriving soon to pick up the day-olds.

"Only if you can help me round out my resume," he said in a serious tone, all sunlight gone from his voice.

She snapped her gaze back at him. Oh. Right. She'd asked people to come in person. Her brain was like a sieve these days, hence the lists. She opened her mouth to reply, but then he ruined the serious effect and chuckled.

"No, really." He smiled broadly, the brightness back. "I'm replying to the ad. The help wanted ad. Especially the baking part. I was looking for the oven." He had a slight musical lilt that evoked Ireland or Scotland. She didn't know her lilts like she knew her chocolate cream and baking flour.

"It's not here." She scanned him up and down from her higher vantage point. The slender man was about her age—in his mid-to-late twenties. He sported a green wool sweater that brought out his sea-green eyes—so striking. Freckles sprinkled across the bridge of his nose and across his cheeks. At the nape of his neck, his curly red hair peeked out under his dark cap.

"Well, with a little more—" He waved his hands around as if he were conjuring up something. "Space, maybe it could." He smiled sheepishly and tucked his hands under his armpits.

"What? Magic?" She wiped the counter, more out of habit than need.

He shrugged and smiled, making a motion across his lips, as if to zip them shut.

"Top secret, eh? What are you, from the Ministry of Magic?" She folded the towel she'd just been using and straightened the paper cups at her elbow.

He laughed—a big laugh for such a slender man—and shook his head. "I wish. Now that would be fun, wouldn't it?" His eyes seemed to sparkle and something about his whole demeanor lit up the cold, blustery morning.

Was that a wink?

She sucked in a breath. She couldn't help but smile back and pause in her multi-tasking busyness. "It would be fun." Magic wasn't real, but it was fun to entertain the possibility. Baking was a sort of magic—that special combination of ingredients, when applied with a little heat, turned into something delicious and evocative.

Though the morning rush was over, a few people were lining up behind this man who made her joke and smile and forget for a moment her lack of employees and her tight cash flow just as her business was getting busier. She had no idea cupcakes would be so popular in the winter.

Her business plan had her estimating that the spring and summer would be her busy seasons and she'd be able to at least break even in the fall and winter. Boy, had she been wrong.

Business was finally picking up after eight months of working her cupcake cart out of San Francisco's Financial District. Her stress level was at an all time high with all the work and her not really properly prepared for it. Success was harder work than she ever expected.

He noticed her looking over his shoulder and motioned for the next person to take his place, a young man in a bike messenger outfit. "Sorry about that sir, what can we get you?" the red-haired man said in his lilt.

"A macchiato and two warmed apple nut cupcakes," the bike messenger said with a half-grin on his face. Another customer was acting uncharacteristically, after all.

"Coming right up," the red-haired man said. He grinned at her, hustled around to the entrance of her cart, and stepped up into it.

The words "get out" died in her throat as she watched him handle the espresso machine like he'd been using it his whole life. He was taller than her by about five inches, but not so tall that he'd butt his head against the ceiling of the cart.

Who did he think he was? She huffed and crossed her arms on her chest. He then handed her the complete order in what seemed like under a minute.

Kate puffed out her irritation. Time to let it go. If he wanted the customer service portion of the job, what better way to test him than let him have a live audition? She could adapt quickly. Soon she didn't feel like she was auditioning him, they had such a smooth operation going.

In between a small cap and three muffin cupcakes to a tourist in an oversized sweatshirt, the Golden Gate Bridge plastered across his chest, she found out her bold helper's name: Florian MacMillian. Between four large lattes and ten savory breakfast cupcakes to four of her regular clients, men and women in their well-tailored business suits, he told her he was from Alaska and needed a job for December he could sink his teeth into to round out his resume.

She laughed at that. He chuckled too. So he was serious about the resume part.

It felt good to laugh. The cart didn't seem so lonely as it had been these last few months as business had started picking up. She didn't realize how much working mostly alone had been weighing on her.

Her one other part-time employee helped a bit, but somehow that woman's presence wasn't the same. Florian really seemed at home in her tiny cart. He efficiently and elegantly made delicious-looking espresso drinks, with full on foam decorations on top. Some were smiley faces, others were Christmas trees and stars, and she thought she saw one with an elf with a bell cap flopped over.

When there was a lull in the service about an hour later, she turned to him. "Can you bake?" She rubbed the knot that had been permanently lodged behind her shoulders for weeks. She really needed some downtime, maybe with some girlfriends at a spa where they served wine.

He smiled at her brightly and handed her a resume from his back jeans pocket. "Of course." He'd slipped off his jacket and cap at some point and was wearing one of her branded aprons over his green sweater. She stared at the cupcake on his chest, broader than she thought it was when he'd been wearing his jacket. She realized she was staring and jumped her gaze to his resume in hand. After perusing it, she glanced back up at him astonished. "Where haven't you been?"

He shrugged, a half smile on his lips. "Well, I'm sure there's some undiscovered pastry gem of a town I haven't visited, say, in the jungles of Brazil." He chuckled.

She glanced back at the resume and sucked in a breath of surprise. "You worked at Giovanna Rosa Leone MacAuley's Italian pastry shop in New York City. I've heard of that place." She couldn't keep the awe out of her voice. "I love their cream puffs at Stella's in North Beach. The amaretto, and the sweetened mascarpone cream, topped with swirls of delicious chocolate mousse and Chantilly cream." She sighed. He might just be the perfect bakery chef for her.

He grinned. "Me too! I got to make those. My sister's fiancé recommended me. Giovanna is his mother, my sister's fiancé. That's how I got that gig. And my mad skills."

"And Paris! You made éclairs in Paris." She sighed again.

"Go where the experts are, my uncle always says."

She nodded and rolled her shoulders to try to relieve the tension lodged there. "Now there's just the matter of the salary and other paper work," she said and handed him a prepared file folder of the employment tax and business forms.

Florian glanced at the little handbook for employees at the top of the stack and looked back up at her. "I prefer to work on a contract basis, if you don't mind. Well, even if you do, that's what I prefer." He kept his tone cordial, but firm.

She eyed him a moment, assessing. She liked his style. Direct and kind. She could work with him. Judging people quickly was part of what had made this type of business a good fit for her.

"Well, if you bake as well as you make espresso, I'm sure something can be arranged."

He brightened. "Then we have a deal." He stuck out his hand to shake.

She gripped his warm palm and smiled at how simple hiring this man seemed. He was sweet, easy to work with, fast, nice to her and customers—so far—and he was cute too. A nice bonus.

His grip was firm, his palm smooth, and long tapered fingers strong around her hand. She didn't want to let go, so she did. She didn't have time for complications as cute as him. She just needed to get her business to the next level.

"We will have a deal when you pass Phase Two, Cupcake Baking 101, and your references check out. Be at the kitchen tomorrow morning, 5 a.m. In Rockridge. Oakland. Across the bridge. Do you know where that is?" She tried not to smile at what felt like a goofy grin blooming on her face.

"Is the test the baking or the arriving on time?" He chuckled.

She laughed, heat blooming on her cheeks. "Yes."

Just then her phone rang again and several more customers lined up at the window. She shrugged and waved at the window and her phone. "This is why I need your help."

"That's why I'm here," Florian said, flashing her a bright smile.

"Thank you," Kate said and answered the phone. "Kate's Cupcakes, Kate speaking."

"Yes, hello, I'd like to know if you have any openings to cater a party in a few weeks, on the twentieth. My nephew is turning six," a man said.

Kate flipped to that page in her agenda, her palm still tingled from Florian's grip.

Someone knocked on the door. She glanced at it, but didn't open it. Florian was still helping customers. The knock came again.

"I do have that date available. I'm going to have to get your number and call you back. We're in the middle of a shift here and—" Kate said.

"Oh, yes, of course." The man gave her his number.

"I'll call you back later today," she said and clicked off her phone.

She grabbed the satchel from the bottom of one of the coolers and then opened the door. "Hey Mike, here's the day-olds from yesterday, and I made you some fresh this morning too."

Mike smiled through his bushy salt-and-pepper beard. He zipped up his faded parka and took the bag full of cupcakes. "Thanks Kate! You're the best. The kids love the flavors you've been sharing. Same time tomorrow?"

"You bet, Mike."

He kissed her on the cheek and patted her shoulder, like a kindly uncle. "You and your staff are invited to our Christmas party on the twenty-first. The kids will be expecting you."

"Of course, I'll come."

Mike squinted at her. "And don't work so hard. You need to take time off to enjoy life. Life isn't all work, you know."

"I know, but things are finally picking up." She stood in the doorway of her cart, rooted to the spot.

"You're doing your best. That's all we ever do." And with that bit of wisdom he hustled back to the family shelter nearby he helped run.

Hope so, but there was so much more to do, always. The never-ending to-do list to keep her on track.

"That's a might nice of you," Florian said, pulling her out of her mental list making.

"No child should go hungry. I do what I can." She shrugged and reached for her agenda to scribble down her list. She knew what it was like to struggle. She put herself through college and had eaten cheap noodles and day-olds for years.

"And you run a busy outfit." Florian scrubbed the espresso machine to gleaming.

"It's been busier than I ever imagined it would be this time of year." Or so soon. She turned back to the counter and wiped it down. Her phone rang again.

"You'll tell them the position is filled, won't you?" Florian said with a false stern look.

She chuckled. "As long as you pass the baking test."

"Oh, I will." Florian smiled, one dimple revealing itself.

She caught herself staring at his mouth. She grabbed her phone just as he stepped to the window to help another customer.

If Florian worked out, she wouldn't need to hire another baker. She'd only need to find one more customer service person as backup and someone to help her with the kids' parties. And get a phone service. She needed to get back to her entrepreneur support group one of these evenings to pick their brains on the best, most affordable options.

She answered the phone. A nearby office wanted a tray of her special gluten-free lunch cupcakes, an assortment of vegetarian and meat. Could she have it ready for tomorrow pick up? She flipped open to an order page in her agenda.

"Yes, I can," she said, while she calculated the extra time she'd need to spend baking tomorrow morning for this order and the ingredients needed. She could swing by the market on her way back to the kitchen this afternoon and get to the kitchen extra early tomorrow.

Juggling a fast-growing business was a good problem to have, she reminded herself. But her professors in the MBA program had never told her how stressful it could be. Or maybe they had and she hadn't been listening, so self-assured she'd been.

She got the details and credit card information. "Please come pick them up at 11 a.m. tomorrow." And clicked off.

She rubbed the knot at her shoulder blade. She could do this, right? And what if this guy didn't work out? She'd be back to square one, struggling mightily to get her business off the ground, by herself, until she found someone else suitable—if she didn't crack first and retreat to her childhood bedroom a twenty-something failure. She shoved the unreasonable panic aside. She had work to do.

Chapter Two

Tuesday, December 2
Rockridge neighborhood, Oakland, CA

The next morning, in her rented kitchen at the back of a wide and busy shopping street, Kate prepped the cupcakes for the day, packing up the travel cases as she went. She rolled her shoulders. She'd slept enough, but the knot in the back of her shoulders was still there.

If Florian didn't work out—she blew out a breath—she'd be ready for the workday, but she'd still be without an extra pair of hands in the kitchen or another helper at the cart. Which she desperately needed. She rolled her shoulders again. She really needed to make time for that massage and spa day and step away from it all. When was the last time she took a real break? She couldn't even remember. She'd been working or going to school for the last seven years, practically non-stop.

If this cute, red-haired man who made her smile, and laugh, didn't work out, she could call all the others. Three more people called in to reply to her ad yesterday while Florian was helping her in the cart. In fact, she probably should call back the qualified ones, just in case, so she could hire a back up, at some point soon.

She jotted down a note in her agenda to call the potential employees back and checked the time on her phone. He would arrive in five minutes, if he wasn't late, and could find her kitchen hidden behind the Dreyers Building off College Avenue.

The phone rang. She answered without checking the caller ID, thinking it was Florian.

"Hello?" Her voice was breathy with anticipation. Her stomach fluttered. Oh dear.

"Oh, hello." A woman chuckled. "Is this Kate Delore?"

"It is." She gulped. Not Florian.

"Sorry for calling so early," the woman barreled ahead, saving Kate from having to explain the way she answered the phone. "I was planning to leave a message. I'm Leslie Winthrop," the woman paused as if Kate should know who she was.

"No, that's okay," Kate finally said, recovering and slipping into her professional phone manner. "I'm an early bird, like many bakers."

"Wonderful." The woman breathed a sigh. "I'd like to hire you for a party next week, Saturday. For my daughter, Amber's ninth birthday party."

Kate blinked. It wasn't typical birthday party season for her business, and yet this was the third request in as many days. Was word getting around? She liked this part of her business, though she had only done a few parties when her business started. In her meager experience, parties were usually a nice bump in cash flow and a nice change of pace.

Kate flipped the pages of her calendar and grabbed a pen. "Saturday next week would work. I request a deposit and a head count a week in advance, so that would be today. Does that work?" Butterflies jumped in her stomach. She was asking for money upfront for parties. A new thing. Always a new thing in this business of hers. That was what she signed up for, right?

The mother eagerly agreed.

A knock sounded at the kitchen door.

Kate opened the door and motioned for Florian to come in, still holding the phone to her ear.

He smiled, nodded, opened his mouth, and then noticing she was on the phone, tied on the apron she handed him, of course with a big cupcake on it.

The mom was telling her how Amber liked chocolate and apples and anything with rainbow sprinkles.

Kate nodded, made agreeing noises, and then handed Florian the to-do list she'd prepared for him, as a way of getting to know his way around the kitchen.

He flashed another charming smile at her, eyed the paper, and gave her a thumbs up. While he wandered off to map the location of all the ingredients, Kate jotted down the mom's cupcake preferences. She pulled out an order sheet from the back of the planner and got the mom's credit card information and head count. Fifteen girls and as many adults. She could do that if she baked Friday after work, and had help with the clean up, and did another supplies run.

Then the mom asked another question, distracting her from her mental to-do list. "Can you do a magic show too? I've asked around and couldn't find anyone for that date. My little girl loves magic shows and—" The mom paused, her breathing hitched. Was she going to cry? "I just don't know what to do."

"Um," Kate hesitated. "I don't generally—I'm usually just doing the cupcakes and coffee, tea, too, if you want."

"I'll make it worth your while. Five hundred dollars extra for a thirty-minute show."

Kate gulped. That would practically double the whole party fee.

Florian open the fridge near her and was pulling out the cold ingredients for the batch she wanted him to make: a fairly easy recipe of apple fritter cupcakes, her own recipe. That was quick. He'd already completed the ingredient map. He moved to the other side of her and pulled out the dry ingredients. It was a small kitchen. All she could afford.

He brushed past her to bring everything to the open counter space.

"You okay?" he whispered.

She nodded and said into the phone. "Leslie, just a minute. Can I put you on hold for a sec?"

"Sure."

Kate stared at Florian, the way he moved with lightness to his step. He was humming under his breath some jaunty Celtic tune.

"Good morning, Florian. Thanks for being on time. Do you do, I mean, can you do magic tricks? It's for a party. Of girls. Little girls. I get asked to bring in a party magician sometimes. As I put in the ad, I cater parties sometimes too."

He peered up from the flour he was measuring, a strange expression on his face, part scared, part guilty, like he'd been found out that he'd eaten all the chocolate. "A party. For girls?"

"Yes, girls. Nine year olds. Is that okay? Next week Saturday."

"I could probably figure something out." He stared down at the bowl of flour.

"You sure? You can work with children."

"Of course. I've done that a lot." Florian blinked at her and smiled, brightening. "I can learn magic tricks. Sure, why not? I'm a fast learner."

Kate breathed a sigh. Florian had only been in her kitchen five minutes and already he was helping her out in ways she didn't even know she needed. She felt like she was walking out over a chasm, the pathway appearing with each new step. It was nerve wracking and a bit exciting. For a moment, she saw herself crossing that bridge hand in hand with Florian. But that was silly. She just met him. She had a business to run. She didn't have time for love. She didn't even have time for a massage.

Florian flashed a smile and turned back to his measuring and his melodic humming. He glanced at her recipe and peered around. He tapped the sheet in front of her. He wanted to know which oven to use. Good question, as this small kitchen had three.

She pointed to the one in the middle.

Florian gave her another thumbs-up and set the oven to pre-heat. He could follow instructions. Another plus in his column. He was just here to bake. That was all.

Kate spoke into the phone. "Leslie, we can do it. I have someone on my team who can do a thirty-minute magic show for the fifteen children at your Amber's ninth birthday next Saturday." She repeated the details for as much the mom's benefit as her own. She wanted clear expectations and everyone knowing what they were getting.

"Is he good with children? You've done a background check, right? You never can be too careful. Why, my neighbor told me this horrible story—"

"Leslie, Mrs. Winthrop," she gently interrupted. "Everything will work out. I'm happy to send you my references, if that will help." She crossed her fingers mentally that Florian's background check would have no red flags.

"Yes, please, even though I have it on good authority that you're wonderful." She chuckled. "Have a very good day, Kate. My Amber will be so happy when I tell her she'll get her favorite cupcakes and a magic show too." She sighed and hung up. She'd forgotten to ask who referred Leslie to her.

Kate jotted down some more planning notes, making calculations about supplies and costs. Even with paying Florian to help, she'd still make a profit.

Maybe things were looking up in her business, after all. She just needed to juggle her tight cash flow with a bit more support, and maybe this crazy, wonderful business would get off the ground.

She slipped her planner back into her satchel and tied on an apron. Time to see what Florian could cook up.

Florian felt right at home in Kate's tiny kitchen, with barely enough room for two people. He moved past her for the flour while she was on the phone and then past her again to bring it back to the mixing bowl. She smelled of lilac and cinnamon. That seemed to capture her nature perfectly, both sweet and spicy. He was intrigued.

But he wasn't here for the conversation, or the intriguing woman he was hopefully going to work for, he reminded himself. He was here to round out his resume, get some final experience, and wow her with his mad skills.

When he started his year away last January, his *Suibhal*, the Christmas elf year abroad, he'd known he'd learn a lot and have a great time in the process, but he hadn't known he'd eventually miss this place.

The human world was infinitely fascinating, not like the enclosed world of the Pole. He'd miss this chaotic, unpredictable place, he realized. But for now he didn't want to think about going home, under four weeks away. All he wanted to focus on was impressing the sweet, spicy Kate with the best apple fritter cupcakes she ever did taste.

He hummed, measured, and stirred, then turned to see Kate watching him.

"About the magic show and the party, I realize I didn't even check your references yet."

"Or taste my baking." He smiled, hoping she'd smile back.

She didn't, but did hand him the baking trays ready with paper cups.

He nodded, took the trays, and deftly poured in the sweet batter. With a little dance to go with his humming, he slid the two trays into the oven and set the timer on his phone.

"And now we wait," he said and spun back to her.

She straightened her face out, but he could tell she'd been smiling.

So it was all business, was it? He could do that. She'd relax once she'd tasted the cupcakes.

He leaned back against the counter. "References, right?"

She nodded. "And experience working with children."

"I thought you might need a references page with my non-baking and cooking experience. You never know." He cracked a smile, slid the sheet of references out of his backpack, handed it to her, and watched her read the two-page document. That should do it nicely.

She glanced up at him. "I saw this on your resume. Your first reference is a Christopher McClenahan at Uncle Chris's Bakery Kitchen in Anchorage for five years before coming down here."

Since it wasn't really a question he just nodded.

"And your experience with children?" She kept reading.

"Listed with the volunteer activities." He stepped to the sink to clean up.

"So every Christmas season you run a day camp for kids," she said without looking up.

He turned on the tap and glanced at her. "Yes, their parents are quite busy that time of year. I've worked with all ages from tot to teen."

She nodded and didn't smile at his alliteration. "I'll need to check these, just as a due diligence."

"Of course. Just check the second page." Florian pointed at the page with a mixing spoon. "I did the work with kids with my brothers. Their numbers are listed. So is Mrs. MacAuley's at the pastry shop in New York City, where we sometimes catered parties. All the other catering jobs were short term, so I don't know if they'll remember me much, and those weren't with kids, per se."

"You sure have done a lot of travelling recently."

She sounded a bit envious.

"I have. All year. It's been great." He grinned and scrubbed the mixing bowl.

"But I need someone here I can count on." She frowned at him.

"Your ad said part-time temporary. How long is that?" He rinsed off the bowl and set it in the drainer.

"Through the Christmas season, at least until December twenty-second or twenty-third. I may close the cart down sooner if business slows down. After that I go on a short break until the start of the New Year."

She frowned and shook her head. She didn't seem pleased at that plan.

Florian wondered which part she didn't like: The break or working almost right up until Christmas. Most chefs he'd worked for during the past year were like Kate; they had a hard time taking breaks away from the business.

"I'm available until the twentieth." He wasn't expected home until the twenty-second to whip up a buffet of delights to wow Uncle, show off all he'd learned, and be awarded his Master Chef hat. He had to be on a plane by the twenty-first and wanted a day to transition.

The buzzer on his phone rang a melodic tune. He opened the oven and checked the cupcakes. A warm, sweet aroma wafted around them. They smelled ready. With the oven mitt, he brought the trays out of the oven and placed them on the counter to cool.

"The proof is in the pudding, or in this case, cupcakes." He chuckled at his own joke.

Kate smiled at him, relaxing her shoulders a little. She inhaled the rich flaky buttery smell and nodded, perhaps unconsciously.

As long as he could keep his magic under control, show up on time, learn a ton, and make Kate smile, he was going to really enjoy his final few weeks of his year abroad. And hopefully Kate would too. He wanted to bring joy with him wherever he went.

Kate filed away his resume and references in her thick calendar. He turned to continue cleaning up his baking area. Joy bubbled up in him like a just-poured glass of soda pop. Before he even was aware of what he was doing, he'd turned on the faucet and floated the mixing spoons into the sink—with a flick of his wrist and just the intention of his runaway magic.

Two things happened at once. His cell phone rang like a school bell, and the spoons clattered into the sink, startling him. "Oh!"

"What?" Kate said. She'd been immersed in her planner, jotting notes, and tapping her pen against the page.

He rushed to the sink and turned off the tap. His heart sped up. Oh no. "I thought I'd get a jump start on the cleaning. You know how it is. Small space, lots of things to wash. Stay on top of it."

Kate eyed him, frowned, and pulled out the ingredients for the next batch of cupcakes.

He swore again to himself. That would be Aunt Holly on the phone. That was her special ringtone she'd programmed in herself and that he couldn't un-program. She was surely scolding him for his use of magic. She always knew. No one explained to him how she knew. And asking her had gotten him nowhere. Now something unexpected was about to happen.

Magic in the mundane world always had unintended and expected consequences.

He was twenty-five years old. He thought by now he'd be able to control his magic. But his year abroad had taught him just the opposite: that he couldn't control his magic and that it always arrived unexpectedly. At least, the consequences had been harmless—so far.

Chapter Three

Kate thought she saw something sparkle out of the corner of her eye when Florian turned on the faucet. But when she looked up it was gone and he was sweeping the floor with brusque movements. He scooped up something sparkly from the floor and dumped it into the trash. Odd.

"Did you break something?" Kate said evenly, stress bubbling below the surface in her chest. She blew out a breath. She really didn't want to fire him, just after he got here, but she would if she had to. Breaking things in her tiny kitchen, her things that she worked hard to buy. She huffed out a breath. She was just overreacting to nothing. The stress was getting to her and it was only Tuesday. She rubbed her temple and told herself to relax. She needed Florian's help, or else she'd be scrambling even more just as business was not only picking up but accelerating.

Florian shook his head, then shrugged and eyed her guiltily. Then nodded. "You're not going to believe this."

"Try me." Kate clenched her jaw then blew out a breath. Stress. Overreacting, remember, she chided herself. Accidents happened in the kitchen. She needed to focus on what was important: tasting his cupcakes. They smelled amazing, better than when she baked them. But she wouldn't let herself be bribed by them. She crossed her arms over her chest and waited, enjoying the sweet, spicy scent of the cupcakes with every inhale, despite her mood. She controlled herself from tapping her foot. Calm down, Kate.

With a smooth movement, Florian expertly lifted a cupcake from the tin and sliced it in half. He held out a half to her, still in its paper wrapping. Sweet tangy aroma of cooked apples had her mouth watering.

He glanced at her. "The wooden stirring spoon—" He frowned and shrugged. "I, uh—"

The cupcake smelled so rich and welcoming. Maybe she could be bribed, a little. Kate picked up her half and nibbled. She sighed and closed her eyes for a moment, enjoying the combination of flaky and tart, the baked apples just the right amount of crunch and soft. Something about having someone else bake for her, especially cupcakes that tasted this delicious, always brought memories of Mom and Grand Mom in the kitchen cozy on Sunday mornings.

Florian paused and watched her. She could feel his gaze on her as she savored the cupcake.

Some pressure released from the tension in her chest. What was she thinking? Of course, she could be bribed. She was hiring him for his baking, after all.

She opened her eyes and watched Florian eat his half. He nodded and hummed.

"The wooden spoon—" She prompted him. She still had to be the boss.

He wiped his hands on his apron. "It—broke. I'll replace it."

"That's what caused the something sparkly where I saw you sweeping?"

"Sorry. I'll replace it," he said again, eyeing the floor where he'd been sweeping, and shook his head.

Kate eyed him and finished her half, all of it, and licked her fingers. Delicious. She gave a little sigh and spoke softly and deliberately. "Spoons are replaceable. And good bakers who show up on time and are good with customers are hard to find."

He snapped his gaze to her. She took an intake of breath to compliment his baking, but he jumped in before she could. "So I passed the test?" He grinned at her, then sobered when she didn't smile back.

More pressure released from Kate's chest. She breathed out as a weight lifted from her shoulders and glanced around her tiny, spotless kitchen. She needed to make a decision, commit. If she wanted to expand her business, she needed to take risks. Hiring Florian seemed risky for some reason she couldn't put her finger on. "I want to say 'yes.' Your baking is good." She eyed her phone. "We have two hours to make three more batches and get on the road to the city. Let's see how the rest of the morning goes."

"I'll take that as a yes."

"For now."

"Where do you want me?" Florian said, eyeing her without his ready smile.

Kate felt something in her chest twinge, not stress this time. Something else. When this man wasn't smiling or exuding his good cheer, he seemed—not ordinary, just not at his best—like a man with a cold. She shook herself mentally and handed him the next recipe, a more complicated one: chocolate croissant cupcake. "I think you're ready for this one."

"So that means I graduated to the next level and have yet another test to pass?"

"Yes." She smiled despite her best efforts, hoping he'd smile back. He was cute when he smiled. He lit up like a Christmas tree. And she liked him. It was nice working with someone who was good and that she liked. Decision made. Something fluttered in her belly. So what if she thought he was attractive. She could keep things professional.

"As long as you can handle the early mornings in the kitchen five days a week, then a busy few hours helping customers, three days a week, you're hired. I pay weekly and don't tolerate tardiness."

"I understand." He held out a hand.

She shook it, one pump European style. Her heart jumped. A tingle of warmth spread up her arm.

Florian grinned. "And thanks! I'll get you a new spoon."

"Yes, please." She glanced in the garbage can, but only saw a pile of sparkles. Strange. But nothing she could do anything about. She had a new employee. Contractor, she corrected herself.

In an hour and a half, they were set up at her spot in downtown San Francisco, and serving customers cupcakes and coffee as if they'd been a team for years.

By 10 a.m. and with no mishaps or blow ups, another layer of stress she'd been holding onto between her shoulder blades rolled off her.

Now she needed to juggle her budget to make sure she could afford the rest of the extra help as her business expanded. Cash flow was tight. She had just enough to cover Florian and supplies with all the new jobs coming in. She didn't want to go into debt, if she could help it. But she knew lots of businesses in the start up phase went into debt so they could expand. Debt financing for expansion made her nervous and tied her stomach up in knots.

She'd come of age just as the economy tanked and watched her parents' savings disappear due to banks mistakes. She'd had to work her way through college and take on student debt, but couldn't get credit cards, due to her parents' situation. It had been just as well. She'd learned to get by. She didn't want to scramble with finding investors or trying to get a business loan. She blew out a breath and stepped up to help the next person in line.

In a lull in the service at 10:45 a.m., Kate turned to Florian. "So about the magic tricks for the party next week, what can you do? Card tricks? Coin out of the ear?"

He shook his head. "None of those."

"Then what?"

"I'm a fast learner. I told you." He smiled brightly.

"So you can't do any? What? You told me you could."

"No, I said that I could figure something out and that I was a fast learner."

The air whooshed out of her. Frustration pressed on her shoulders. She was forgetting things that only happened a few hours ago previous. She didn't like it that she couldn't hold on to the details.

"Right." She rolled her shoulders, trying to relieve some of the tension always there beneath the surface. "What am I going to do?"

"What do you mean?"

"If you can't learn the tricks, I'll have to call the mother back, refund her money—" She scrubbed the already spotless counter.

"Whoa. Wait. You're jumping ahead of the sleigh there. I said I can do this. We can do this."

She glanced at him. "What do you mean 'we'? I'd be out a lot of money."

He reached out to touch her arm, but stopped short. "I mean you and I." He gestured between them.

"But I don't know how to do magic tricks. I'm relying on you." She stomped her foot and crossed her arms, feeling unreasonable. Just as things were looking up in her business, now the truth that Florian didn't actually know how to do magic tricks tipped her over the edge. Where was she this morning? Oh, trying to close a deal over the phone. She rubbed her temples. She really needed a break.

He wiped down the espresso machine, already gleaming, then turned to her with a calming smile. "Listen, Kate, we'll figure it out. Promise. I really am a fast learner. I'd never baked cupcakes before today, but they came out great, right?"

"What? Really! They were—" She sighed. "Fantastic."

"See?" He crossed his arms too and gave her a mock frown.

Kate smiled and eyed him sideways and then turned to watch the pedestrians clip by outside her little cupcake stand window. "I need to know I can rely on you."

She glanced at him. He looked so open and eager, with a ready willingness to help her. Why was that? She shook herself.

It didn't matter why. What mattered was that he was here now. He was working for her. He was a good sport. So ready to leap into the unknown. For a moment, she wished for some of that readiness. She'd been so methodical, step-by-step with the business, only leaping as circumstances warranted it. But hiring him felt like a risk, so she had to be heading in the right direction, right?

She straightened. She could leap, a little. "I—we need to practice, learn, prepare. As soon as possible. Let's meet tonight." She felt a shy smile bloom on her face.

"You must really like me to want to see so much of me." He joked and shook his head. The red curls swung at the nape of his neck.

She caught herself staring at said neck and brought her gaze back to his. "You're nice to look at."

"And I bake good too." He smiled like he knew she'd been staring.

"Well." She folded the hand towel again. Flirting with the help. Luckily, a woman in a tailored business suit stepped up to the window. Kate turned to take her order.

"Things will work out, you'll see," Florian said and touched her arm.

They'd better. If she couldn't manage this growth spurt, she'd have to re-evaluate everything: her life, her business, and go back to square one.

"What would you like?" Kate asked her customer.

Kate rubbed her arm. Was that a zap of warmth flowing up her arm where Florian had touched her? No, it couldn't be. Yet an image of his arms around her, enveloping her in warmth, swamped her. Her imagination was working overtime, just like she was.

Chapter Four

Later that evening, Florian stood outside her door for five minutes, since he was early, and wondered how he was going to handle his wayward magic. He rubbed his chilled hands together. The temperature had dropped dramatically. He'd need gloves if this weather kept up.

His aunt's stern message the day before, which he'd finally listened to in the afternoon, warned him yet again against using magic. Unintended consequences, someone could get hurt, he couldn't reveal who he was or else, etc. and etc. He understood, but it was getting harder to control his magic, not easier, and no one had prepared him for that. How could they? Most elves returned to the Pole after their year abroad and never talked about their experiences. And the few that didn't return like his Aunt Holly didn't talk about magic in the Human world either, since they'd given it up.

He shivered at that thought. He didn't want to give up his magic. He loved the rush, and he especially loved the joy that sparked the flow of magic through his veins. He knew intellectually that joy and magic didn't have to be paired, but for him they were.

Florian knocked on Kate's apartment door. He needed to control his magic, he reminded himself, for the umpteenth time. But something about being around Kate just brought it more out of him.

A moment later, she answered and waved him in to her entryway. She padded to a small kitchen that opened directly into a living room. He followed to stand in the cozy living room.

"Make yourself at home," she said and opened the refrigerator. "Would you like something to drink?"

He smiled at her. "Sure. Whatever you're having."

She looked lovely, her chestnut hair streaked with chic green and done up in a casual ponytail. She also looked huggable in her russet-colored fuzzy sweater over jeans. The sweater covered her hips and hung down to her thighs. He turned to peruse her place so he wouldn't keep staring at her.

"Take off your coat and stay a while." There was a smile in her voice. She sounded the most relaxed he'd seen her so far. He liked this relaxed version of Kate, too. He liked all the versions of Kate he'd seen.

"No, I'm good." If he took off his coat, he'd have to take off his hat and he wasn't warm enough to do that.

"Have a seat. I'm just getting us some wine."

He took a few steps into the living room with a red plushy love seat and matching easy chair. A long low table completed the ensemble. No TV. A small speaker system nestled in between books on a full to overflowing bookshelf.

He chose the love seat. Maybe she'd join him and they could do more than just practice for the magic show. He shook his head. He was going home soon. He didn't want to start anything now.

She returned with a bottle of red in one hand and two wine glasses in the other. "You okay?" She asked.

"Yah, yes. Fine." Florian rubbed his hands. He was warming up.

"You're a bad liar." She set down the wine and glasses. "You look nervous about the magic show. I'm nervous too. Did you bring the list of magic tricks?" She poured herself a glass and left the empty glass in front of him as an open invitation.

She sat in the easy chair.

He pulled folded pieces of paper from his back pocket. "Straight to business, then." He unfolded the paper and handed her one. "I made a duplicate."

She read the paper and frowned. "You can do all these?"

He nodded. "That's the idea."

She squinted up at him. "That's not an answer." She shook a finger at him, trying not to smile. "I'm getting to know your slippery ways."

Florian shrugged. "Okay. I watched all of the tricks on YouTube. I'm a fast learner. Remember?"

"Let's see."

Florian swallowed. He was prepared for this, but still his nerves jangled like out-of-tune elf hat bells. He stood and faced her. From his other back pocket, he pulled a deck of cards. He fanned them out and offered them to her.

"Pick a card and look at it. And don't tell me what it is."

Kate nodded, danced her fingers across the deck, and then slipped one out. She peeked at it and sipped some wine. She eyed him solemnly.

"You've memorized it?" Florian asked.

Kate nodded.

"Slip it back into the deck. I won't look." He closed his eyes. "And let me know when you're done.

Would this work?

"Done," Kate said.

Florian opened his eyes. "Now I will shuffle the deck and find your card."

Kate frowned.

"Seems impossible, doesn't it?" He paused.

Kate nodded. "You want me to pretend I'm a nine year old girl who loves magic shows."

"Yes, please. That would help with verisimilitude."

"Making it real."

"Yes, that too."

That got her to smile.

"So, that seems impossible, right?" he said again.

"Yes!" Kate said and pumped her fist in the air with child-like enthusiasm.

"If I can find your card in three tries or less, then you have to do a card trick too for all your friends."

Kate cocked her head sideways. "You're going to ask a nine-year-old to do a card trick in front of her friends?"

"Yes, is that too much?"

"Well, she might be shy."

"Really?"

"Yes." Kate sobered and sipped her wine.

"Okay. What could work? What could be a reward if I get it right?"

"Applause should be enough."

"But there needs to be something at stake."

"For who? I'm confused. Can you find the card or not? Let's just see if you can do the trick. Because if you can't—" She shook her head and took a big gulp of wine.

He knew the stakes. She'd have to refund the money or find someone else, both of which would add to her already full plate. He saw how hard she worked, as hard or harder than any of his elf brethren, himself included. But she had the added weight of running the whole show herself. At least where he came from there was at least 1,500 elves working together in a highly choreographed harmony.

He cleared his throat dramatically. "Did you know that there are 586 ways to shuffle a deck?"

He didn't give her time to respond, just started counting and doing fun shuffles, without magic—flying the cards between his hands a foot apart; above his head; behind his back; under one leg and then another. When he started on shuffle seven—behind both his legs, Kate chuckled.

He looked up. He'd been concentrating hard and sweating a little under his hat and coat. He was pretty dexterous but these tricks required all of his attention. He'd have to learn to interact more with his audience. Kids had short attention spans after all.

She saluted him with her glass, nearly empty of the pungent fruity red wine. "You'll never find my card now!"

"I will." He set the deck down. "But first, I need to get more comfortable. Card tricks are hard work." He wiped the back of his hand across his brow over-dramatically.

Kate smiled and he slipped off his coat and hung it on the coat tree beside the door. He stuffed his hat in a pocket. He drew his fingers through his hair, to confirm what he already could feel: that his ears were back to their Human rounded shape. They became pointy when the temperature was close to freezing.

"Warmed up?" Kate asked and sipped her wine.

"All warmed up." He picked the deck back up. "You've been watching this? Making sure no one has monkeyed with it?"

"I have." She had her gaze on him, waiting, her cheeks red. Was she blushing? Most alluring.

"You've been watching me and not the deck," he said, eyeing her full lips.

"Guilty as charged." Her blush deepened.

He chuckled and cut the deck, and held it out in front of him, like two clam shells. "That's okay. The deck was safe." He held still for a beat, and then felt through the cards, his sensitive finger pads feeling for her card. He pulled a card out and held it out to her, without looking at it. "Is this it?"

She shook her head. "No," a half-smile on her lips.

He frowned, put the card in his shirt pocket, and felt through the deck. "This one?"

She giggled and poured herself another glass of wine. "Nope."

"Hmm. Really?" He shrugged. "Okay." He slipped that card into his shirt pocket too and walked his fingers across the backs of the cards.

He had her attention now. He had to find the card in this third try or ruin the trick. The tiny mark he'd pushed into the card, he couldn't find. He rubbed the cards between his palms, to better feel the entire card. He felt a tiny nick. This had to be it.

"Here you go." He held up the card for her to see.

She clapped her hands with delight. "You did it. Yes, that's it. The two of hearts."

She stared at him and blushed again. Then took a sip of wine. "What other tricks can you do?" She glanced at her phone. "That was only four or five minutes. You'll need at least five more about that length."

Florian blew out a breath. He could do this, without his elf magic, if the delectable Kate Delore didn't distract him completely.

Chapter Five

Wednesday, December 3
Oakland, CA

The next morning Kate arrived at the kitchen at the lovely hour of 4 a.m., as always, but this time the pre-dawn darkness was too dark, felt too early. She'd had one glass too many the night before. She'd been so nervous about relying on Florian, even though she tried not to show it, she'd gulped down four glasses of wine instead of her leisurely two. Now she had a hangover pounding on her temples for her worries. But Florian had done fine. Better than fine. He'd charmed her, and made her feel warm and fuzzy inside. That couldn't have been just the wine.

She rubbed her temples—the headache meds should kick in any moment now—and fired up her tiny espresso machine. Her parents had given her this wonderful high-end device as a college graduation present—so sweet of them. She kept it at the kitchen instead of at home to motivate her to get to the kitchen this early.

By the time Florian arrived at 5 a.m., her headache was mostly gone and she was on her third espresso. She'd already done all the prep and baked the first four batches of the day's wares. He greeted her and got to work without his customary cheery chatter or bright smile. She was fine with that. Her aching head was fine with that. But a part of her wondered what happened to her cheery helper. It didn't matter, another part of her whispered. They both had a job to do and they did it nicely. Without any chit chat—Florian knew where everything was and started in on the recipe she laid out for them—they settled into a nice rhythm, with her packing up the van and organizing supplies, while he baked and cleaned as he went.

About twenty minutes later, a knocked sounded on the door, and her brother Hank stepped in without waiting for her to invite him in. Of course he would. She kept the door unlocked so she could easily go back and forth between the kitchen and the van in the parking lot.

"Hey sis." He kissed her on the cheek. "Hey." He stuck out his hand to shake Florian's hand.

Florian cracked the first smile she'd seen this morning and gave her brother an elbow to shake, since his hands were covered in dough.

Hank chuckled. Florian did too, and Hank nodded. "I'm Hank Delore, Kate's annoying intrepid younger brother. Or cupcake mooch. Whichever you prefer."

"Intrepid. Nice word." Florian nodded in approval. "You'll have to taste one of mine and tell me what you think. The customers can't tell the difference. But maybe you can." He smiled. "I'm Florian MacMillian, intrepid baker and magic trick doer extraordinaire."

"Doer, huh? She tried to get me to do magic tricks a while back. You're a better man than I, Florian, but 'intrepid,' that's my word."

"I'm borrowing it. I'll give it back."

"I like you." Hank smiled and glanced at her. "I like this guy." He squinted at Florian. "You're going to stick around for a bit?"

"I plan to. For the season," Florian said.

"My sister can be a bit—fierce."

"Hey," Kate said loudly. "I'm not fierce, I'm just driven." She shook her head in mock outrage. "You know we need to get on the road soon. What's up? Did you just stop by to give me a hard time?" She grabbed a large box of day olds for Mike and headed for the door.

"Always," Hank said and glanced at the box with the see-through top. "No reject cupcakes for me this morning?"

"No, we're just about all packed up." She turned to him and swatted at his outstretched hand. "Hey, these are for Mike."

"Yah, okay. I'll come by the cart after finals, next week probably. For fortifications. And because the team wants to taste your latest. But that's not why I came by."

"Spill it, Hank. We're not exactly on your home-to-swim practice route," Kate said, stuffing her bag with her planner and water bottle. One more batch to come out of the oven, Florian to finish cleaning, and they could hit the road, and hopefully miss a good chunk of the traffic over the bridge. "But you can bring the gang by anytime. We should have enough for the whole swim team. I double the lunch orders now. Things are really picking up." That was a good thing, she reminded herself.

"That's great, sis!" He squinted at her, like he wanted to say something else about that, but then grinned. "I stopped by to invite you in person to our annual Christmas-Hanukah-Solstice-Kwanza bash. Friday night. It'll be fun! You too, Florian."

"And you came by to see if you could mooch pastries," Kate said.

"One can always hope!" Hank shrugged.

Florian nodded, up to his elbows in suds at the sink. "Thanks for the party invitation. A bit early, no? For a Christmas party, I mean."

Hank grinned. "The semester ends next week. At Cal. UC Berkeley." He chuckled at Florian quizzical look. "University of California, at Berkeley. You're not from around here, are you? Scotland? The Highlands?"

Florian chuckled. "I get that a lot. No, Alaska. But ancestors are from there."

"Lots of Scots up in Alaska. I had no idea." Hank grinned. "Cool."

Florian nodded and turned on the water to rinse. Kate stepped to the van with her box and hustled back to the kitchen for one last check. She scanned the counters. All clean. She glanced at the time. Five more minutes and they could get on the road.

"Hank, you came all the way down here to tell me that." She elbowed him in the ribs. "You could have called." She liked giving her little brother a hard time, but truth was the only time she saw him lately was when he stopped by for one of his impromptu mooch-cupcake visits.

"I heard you had new help." He grinned, like it was his job to check in on her. Then he shrugged. "I didn't know when I'd get over the bridge, what with swim practice and finals."

"Spying on me then." She swatted his shoulder. "Who did you hear from? I didn't see any of your friends at the cart."

"Mike is friends with our new house leader at the frat house. You'll meet him and his fiancée at the party." Hank leaned in and said loudly. "Bring your new baker."

"I'll come," Florian said, turned off the water, dried his hands, and opened the oven just as the ringer dinged, all in one graceful movement.

Kate caught herself staring. Stop that, she reprimanded herself.

"I'll bring Kate." He winked at Kate. "Maybe show off a few magic tricks before the big day. Like a live rehearsal. Hey, that'd be fun. Wouldn't that be fun, Kate?" Florian grinned at her and set to cool on the rack the final tray of ham and cheese cupcakes with Asiago.

Heat crept into her cheeks. She turned toward the cupcakes, just as a spark shot out of the top of the stove with a loud pop. In microsecond succession, Florian's phone rang an annoying school bell tone.

Kate jumped at the one-two bursts of sound. "What was that?"

Florian flapped a dishtowel on the stove top and swore. "No flames. Nothing." He said something under his breath, and Kate thought she heard his voice shake.

She grabbed the fire extinguisher from off the wall and rushed over to the stove. All the burners and the stove were off. She checked the narrow space between the wall and the stove.

Everything looked connected, as it should be. She waited a beat and nothing happened. So weird. She eyed the time on her phone. They had to get on the road now. She'd have to call the owner to let him know, in case there was a bigger problem in the gas pipes or with the boiler in the building. Her temples pounded, her headache back, as if it had never left. If it wasn't one thing, it was another. The storm of her stress was rising.

"We need to go now." She shoved Hank out the door.

"You'll come, right?" Hank asked, glancing back at Florian, a worried expression on his face, and then at Kate. "You guys all right?"

"We're fine. Just busy. On a schedule. Come on, Hank," Kate said.

"It's all good in here." Florian scooped up the last batch of cupcakes into its box. "I got this." He followed Kate out the door. He placed the box in the back of the van, shut and bolted the back door. He stood there watching her, a serious look on his face, like he wanted to say something. Then he hopped in the passenger seat and shut the door.

Hank stood there beside the van, waiting, frowning.

"What, baby brother?" she said impatiently.

Hank put a hand on her shoulder. He looked down a little at her in his six-foot plus frame. Just a tiny bit taller than Florian, she realized. "I want you to come to the party and not stay at home with a glass of wine and a book. You need a break. You need to relax, you know, laugh, play. With other people. Besides, it's Friday night."

She huffed out a breath, let her shoulders drop, and kissed him on the cheek. "You're right, little brother. I do need time off. I know. I'll bring myself. Florian will bring himself. And I'll bring my favorite bottle of wine. And a book, in case I don't feel like talking to your rowdy fraternity brothers."

"Rowdy, really." He gave her a lopsided grin.

"Okay, loud." She smiled back.

"Maybe, when we're all in one room. Otherwise we're quiet, studious, brilliant, faithful, upright, a credit to society, heroic in everyday ways to serve humanity in every way we can, from now until all the triune lost ones have been found."

Kate said the last few words of his fraternity's pledge with him, even though she had no idea what they meant, and grinned back. She'd only heard it a bazillion times over the last three and a half years Hank had been in his fraternity. She kissed him on the cheek again and chuckled. "Gotta go, baby brother. Good luck with your finals."

"Don't need luck. I have smarts." Hank tapped his temple with two fingers, then kissed his fingers, and touch his heart with them, in a gesture she'd seen him do many times. Some kind of fraternity salute.

She slipped into the front seat of her van and called out through the open door to her baby brother. "Swear you're not trying to set me up with some grad student like last time, and I'll bring a batch of my new Christmas cupcakes."

Hank placed a hand over his heart. "I swear, big sister."

Kate shook her head, shut the door, gunned the engine, and headed out of the parking lot. She navigated onto Chabot Road, and then turned on Claremont toward the freeway.

After a few minutes, Florian said, "Sorry about that."

"For what?" She glanced at him and then back at the morning freeway traffic, luckily still light.

When he didn't answer, she glanced at him again. He was frowning.

She didn't press.

When they got to the tollbooth, she had to slow down due to the traffic back up. She took the opportunity to glance at Florian again. She didn't want to be concerned for him. He could take care of himself, and she had a business to run, but he was unusually silent. And she did care that the people she worked with were—she searched for the word—content with what they were doing for her.

"What's up?" she took the casual tone she usually took with her brother. She wouldn't get attached. Her business was her first, main, and sole focus.

But why couldn't she have other focuses and still run the business? A voice whispered.

He shook his head. "The stove. I must—I thought I turned it off."

"You did. I checked. Maybe it's the gas pipes."

"I hope so." Florian blew out a breath. He turned his phone over and over in his hand with his long, tapered fingers.

Maybe he was nervous about the children's party on Saturday. He'd done fine with all the magic tricks he'd practiced with her the previous night, even got her laughing and blushing and enjoying more wine than usual.

Maybe she'd actually been enjoying herself and that was why she'd had the extra wine. She also blew out a breath and glanced at him again as she drove the van through the tollbooth. Traffic picked up again on the bridge and was moving smoothly, though not as fast as she'd like.

"We'll figure it out," she said.

He nodded and flashed her a bright smile. "Thanks Kate."

Her heart sped up. "For what?"

"For being your brilliant self."

A laugh burst out of her. "Where does that come from?"

"Despite the—hard work, early hours, stress—" He waved his hand in front of him. "I'm having a great time and learning so much."

Kate watched the road. "You're welcome. I think." She smiled. Maybe she could learn something from him too. She could pick his brain about all those places he'd worked. She ignored the heat bursting in her belly. Not that kind of learning, she scolded herself. But she couldn't stop smiling as she took the first exit off the bridge and navigated the van into the city.

Chapter Six

As usual they were busy from 7 a.m. to 9 a.m. The phone kept ringing too, but Kate didn't want to stop serving her hungry customers to get the phone. She'd cancelled the "Help Wanted" ad, so hopefully it wasn't that.

Finally there was a slow down at 9:30 a.m. She sent Florian out for a break and checked her messages.

Two nearby offices were calling in party orders for Thursday and Friday this week, and two more for the following week, and one for two weeks out. Wow! She shook her head and smiled as she scribbled their orders down in her planner and order sheets. Word was getting around. When she started her business in the spring, she had no idea that the Christmas holiday time would be her busiest time. A good problem to have, her business professors would say.

Florian stepped back in. "Your turn. I'll cover things while you take your break."

She nodded thoughtfully and touched his arm. She could use a good stretch of the legs. "Thanks."

He grinned. "Sure thing."

She stared at him, without really seeing him. Just enjoying the feel of his strong arm under her palm. She took in a deep breath. Cinnamon and ginger. She leaned in to smell him more. His reddish wavy hair tickled her nose.

He gripped her shoulders with both hands and leaned toward her. Her breathing hitched. His lips, ripe for tasting, right there.

"Hey lovers."

Kate jumped and dropped her hand from Florian's shoulder, where it had wandered.

At the same time, Florian glanced at the speaker, pulled away from Kate, and exclaimed. "Dahlia! What are you doing here? I thought you were—" he waved his hand. "With your guy."

She laughed. "His name is Liam, little brother."

He narrowed his eyes at the pretty woman with shoulder length bright hair, wavy, the same red color as his own. "I know. I was testing you."

Dahlia laughed. "Introduce me," she said in a loud whisper.

Kate blinked. Her cheeks heated, again. She glanced at Florian.

He looked at her, like he was star struck, and then blinked, and recovered his ready smile. "Dahlia, please meet my boss, Kate Delore, proprietor of this lovely establishment."

Dahlia held up a dainty hand.

Kate shook her hand, surprised at the strength of her grip.

"Nice to meet you, Kate."

"Likewise," Kate said.

Florian continued. "Kate, this is my older sister, Dahlia MacMillian. One of them anyway."

How many sisters did he have? The flood of desire to know everything about him washed over her. She gulped, untied her apron, and hung it up.

"Nice to meet you, Dahlia. Florian can help you out. I need to take my break." Kate nodded at them both and stepped out of the cart. She took long strides up the street and around the corner, circling the block.

Falling for Florian. Oh no. She didn't date employees, no matter how good they smelled or how they made her life more interesting and fun. She had plenty interesting in her life, though she didn't have a lot of fun these days. She'd have fun once she got her business on solid ground. Whenever that would be.

By the time she was back, the pretty bright Dahlia was gone and Florian was making an espresso drink for a customer. Another person was waiting in line. She tied on her apron and nodded to the next customer in line, a young man in a suit. She recognized him. One of her nice handful of regulars. She smiled. "What can I get you?"

"Do you have any of your Asiago ham and cheese cupcakes left?"

She smiled. "For you, always."

Whoa. She was flirting with customers now. Oh dear. Or, oh good. She glanced at Florian. Being around him just these two plus days had already relaxed her, so she was enjoying life a bit more. Flirting, really?! Her mother would not recognize the serious studious child she'd been. How could one person affect her so quickly?

She couldn't blame it on the wine anymore. She was quite sober.

She served the young man.

"Kate, you're the best." He stuffed a few bills in the tip jar. "Hey, are you free Friday night?"

"Why?"

He shrugged. "Maybe we could do drinks at Varia." That new restaurant near the Ferry Building.

"No, she's busy," Florian said. "Whatcha—"

"Hey," Kate glared at Florian and touched his arm to stop him from saying more. "I can speak for myself, thank you very much."

"I know." Florian said. "I'm just looking out for you."

"Uh, that's okay," the young man said. "Maybe another time." He shrugged. Then he looked at Florian. "Lucky, man. See you, Kate."

Kate nodded. "Bye." She turned to Florian. "Friday is not a date."

"I know that. But you are busy."

"Florian, I can speak for myself. And another thing—" She glanced out the window. No one was in line.

He stuck his hands into his jean pockets and leaned against the back counter.

Why did he have to look sexy in that "devil-may-care" pose? Her cheeks flamed again and her heart sped up. "I don't date employees." Stupid rule, her libido whispered to her.

When was the last time she even had a wonderful date that ended in something more than a wave good night? Last year, maybe, right after she'd finished her MBA, with Alex right before he left to pursue his PhD at Oxford. She hadn't even thought about him in months. She'd been too busy with her business, just like she'd thought she'd be.

She'd been happy or at least content with it all—her little burgeoning business kept her plenty busy, thank you very much, with her cash flow stresses and all. The stress came with the choices she'd made to bootstrap her business and build it from the ground up without partners or crowd funding. Her professors had advised against it, but she wanted to do things her own way.

Then Florian stepped into her kitchen and started stirring the pot, awakening desires she'd shelved and forgotten about, like a stash of hidden chocolates. No, it wasn't his fault. She had needs, like every healthy twenty-five year old woman—needs that she pretended she didn't have.

Someone stepped up to the window and her phone rang. She waved Florian to help the customer. She'd take the call. Maybe it was another office calling in a Christmas order.

"Hello, I hear you're doing holiday cupcake parties and magic shows for kids. Are you available a week from this Saturday, in the afternoon?"

"Uh, hello, yes, let me check my calendar." She hadn't even done her first magic show cupcake party and already the word was getting around. Word-of-mom was a powerful thing.

She flipped open her planner. That day she'd only planned to fiddle with some new recipes for the coming week, sleep in, if she could, and go supplies shopping. "Yes, I have that date open." She needed to see if Florian was available that day too. "One moment, Ms.—?"

"Mrs. Lee." the mother said. "Jane Lee. Oh, there will be twelve children and probably five adults. Emily likes sweet sticky buns. Can you make those into cupcakes? Your site says you do special orders. Also, fried banana." Like desserts at Chinese restaurants. Kate had eaten those sweet, sticky pastries before. "Yes, we can do that, if you give us the ingredients list."

"Oh, thank you. And for the magic show, Emily would love something with clowns and balloons. She's six. It doesn't have to be complicated."

Kate nodded. That was a lot of special requests. She calculated supplies cost and time in her head. And the cost to have Florian's help, hopefully.

"Ms. Delore, are you there?" Mrs. Lee said politely, a little worry in her tone.

"Yes, um, one moment, please." She put Mrs. Lee on hold.

Florian was running the espresso machine, so she waited for a moment until he was done foaming the milk. The tiny oven dinged, and he handed the customer, a woman in a fur coat, her Asiago cupcake and latte.

"Florian, are you free next week Saturday for another magic show cupcake party?"

He turned to her, eyed her lips, and then looked her in the eye. "Yes."

"I'll pay you well."

"Okay."

She eyed him for a moment longer. He seemed tense. "You okay?" Her concern for him just slipped out. She didn't want to care, but he seemed subdued, not his usual bubbly cheery self. Why she thought she knew him after spending almost twenty hours with him in the two plus days, she didn't know? But that was a lot of time.

"Yah, fine."

Another customer stepped up to the window, a woman with two children beside her. Florian helped them in his friendly manner, back to his smiling, joking self.

Kate got back on the phone. "Yes, we can help you, Mrs. Lee. Let me call you back with a quote in—" A line was forming. The lunch rush. "In about two hours."

"That's fine. I'm so glad you are available. I just love your combination of creative cupcakes and magic show."

"I'm so glad." Really she was. The word was getting around. "Mrs. Lee, I need to go. Sorry. It's busy here."

"I understand. Many hungry customers." Mrs. Lee chuckled and hung up.

More good problems to have. She blew out a breath and rolled her shoulders. She liked being busy, but why did she feel like something was missing from her life still? She watched Florian smile and joke with customers, learning their names, and making them feel at home.

She gulped and hurried to fill the order he called out. She was fine with not being the front person for a change. She didn't have to do everything herself, she chided. Her business professors would agree, especially if she wanted to build this business into an empire. But did she really want that still? She glanced at Florian and glanced away.

Chapter Seven

After work, Florian helped Kate clean up the cart to gleaming. With few words, they cleaned the espresso machine, refrigerator, and supply shelves. They worked together well. There was always a certain camaraderie with people who worked in the food industry—hard workers all, and with Kate it was no exception. He relaxed into the scrubbing and appreciated that Kate didn't want to chat. He needed the quiet to ruminate on what his sister had said.

He helped Kate pack up the van, haul and stow the cart to its spot in the parking lot garage, and then drove back with her to the tiny kitchen in Oakland to unpack the van. Quietly, they unpacked the trays and boxes into the kitchen, with Kate pointing out what items went where in the large refrigerators. Kate stayed quiet. He was glad for it.

Other than that, after Kate had asked him if he was okay, back at the cart, right after his sister had stopped by, he hadn't known what to say. He couldn't reveal that his sister scolded him for using his magic too much and potentially causing mishaps to Humans and revealing his true identity, losing all he'd worked so hard for. When he'd opened his mouth to protest, she gave him that eagle-eyed glare that missed nothing. He'd snapped his mouth shut so fast his jaw hurt. What could he say to his sister in defense of his actions? She was right. The last thing in the world he wanted to do was cause harm to Humans or reveal his true identity and lose it all.

He couldn't tell Kate either that his aunt called him the moment he used magic. How in the all bells halls did she know so quickly? He had the sinking feeling that the more time he spent with Kate, the more his wild and unpredictable magic would slip out, causing more than kitchen mishaps, sparkles, and mild embarrassment.

But he realized he really liked hearing Kate laugh, and being a part of helping that happen. More than anyone he'd been around. Yes, he'd been bouncing around the country this past year partly because his magic would slip out in weird ways and then he'd have to find an excuse to leave, but also because he was having fun, learning all he could. He was a fast learner. It was easy to feel done with all he could learn in one place, and then move on to the next gig.

Sometimes his magic had slipped out in the past because he was enjoying himself with a woman. No one expected elves to be celibate on their year abroad. But no one was supposed to fall in love with a Human. Everyone was supposed to come home and eventually marry into the clan. Lately though, things had been changing. His sister Dahlia was with a Human and got to keep her status, and then there was Aunt Holly, who gave up her elf life for Uncle John, yet exhibited uncanny abilities.

Sometimes the magic slipped out because he was having so much fun baking in the kitchen, learning new things, and making new creations. Then he'd need to leave soon because his magic would slip into the pastries, and people would come back to the shop, reporting incredible things. He never wanted those things traced back to him and the weird mishaps in the kitchen, so he'd found a way to go to the next gig without fuss. But he didn't want to leave this gig early. It was his last one. And Kate—she drew him, unlike anyone had before. He sighed, placing a stack of trays on a top shelf, and headed back to the van for the last batch of trays.

"Earth to Florian. Hello?" Kate said, jolting him out of his reverie.

Florian was standing in the parking lot, a batch of trays stacked up in his arms.

"Oh, right." He carried the trays into the kitchen. He didn't know what to do. He couldn't control his magic and he didn't want to leave this job, especially since it had just begun. He could see how much Kate needed his help, and how much he was already making a difference to the business and to her. He just had to be more careful, rein in his enthusiasm.

When all the trays and supplies were washed and stored, Florian turned to Kate. "Same time tomorrow morning?"

He just had do his best to control his magic and hope that it wouldn't cause anyone any harm. And that he wouldn't accidentally out himself.

"Actually can you make it a little earlier, at 4:30 a.m., instead of 5 a.m.? We need to bake a bit more for the special orders tomorrow and Friday," Kate looked down at her planner. "Two dozen of the Asiago ham and cheese, half gluten free. Those have been a big hit this week. And three dozen of the garlic roasted vegetable, also half gluten free. That was last week's lunch special." She peered up at him. "Thanks for all your hard work. I really appreciate it." She stepped toward him.

"Sure thing." He stepped back to grab the towel and dry his hands. He glanced around the kitchen. Everything was in its place. "And yes, 4:30 am is fine. But you don't need me for the day shift because you have someone, right? Friday too?"

She flushed and looked like she was going to say something else.

He waved good-bye and stepped out into the cool afternoon air before Kate could ask him again what was up with him. Or before he could kiss her. Oh seven brothers.

Florian rode the train back to his aunt's apartment in San Francisco's Potrero neighborhood. He stared out the window, not seeing anything. He was really enjoying his time with Kate, in addition to all the good baking experience he was getting. There was no question he'd get his Master's badge and cap with all the experience he'd accumulated this year. But he was getting attached to Kate. She was brilliant in her recipes, gutsy to start her own company, smart, and fiery personality masked with orneriness. And those kissable lips and sassy smile. He loved her vibrancy and liked her—a lot. But soon he'd have to leave her to go back home. And not return until the next sanctioned break in ten years hence.

In a daze, he let himself into Aunt Holly's apartment. All his jobs this year had been short term. He'd not felt sad about that until now. Now he felt something more for Kate than just enjoying learning from her. Oh bells.

"Hey, Florian, Want one? Ham and cheese?" Uncle John smiled and waved a fat sandwich in front of Florian, by way of a greeting. Uncle John leaned against the kitchen counter in front of sandwich fixings. Aunt Holly must still be at work.

Florian slid into the small dining table nook at the window. "No thanks. That's what I had for lunch."

"At your new job at the food cart? How's that going?"

"Good."

"But?"

Florian looked at his kind uncle and shrugged. "Nothing."

"Girl trouble?" Uncle John took a big bite of his sandwich. He chewed and eyed Florian. "You're due to go back home soon, right?" It was a relief that Uncle John knew what he was, though they'd never talked about it. His aunt had told him. Florian wasn't the first nephew or niece to couch surf here over the years or stop by for some familial advice.

Florian nodded. He wished he had the desire to drink, or smoke. But he'd never been into those things that could help him forget his troubles for a while. He had to face things straight on.

"Let me guess," Uncle John said. "You're having mixed feelings about going home."

"Something like that." He got up to get a glass of water. Maybe a good fast walk up some of San Francisco's famously steep hills would help him clear his head, and heart.

"And you need to talk to Holly to sort it out because only she will understand."

Florian chuckled.

"Glad to see your humor is back. Do you know it's like you bring the fog indoors when you have the blues?"

"Really? I hadn't realized." Florian gulped down his water. "I think a walk will clear my head. Then I have to turn in. Kate wants me at the kitchen at 4:30 a.m., but I want to be there by 4 a.m. to help her out."

"What if she doesn't want to pay you for that extra time?"

Uncle John, ever the practical one. He was an engineer, after all.

"You know I didn't take the job for the money. I saved plenty from all my jobs this year."

"Seems like you're decided, after all."

"About what?"

"You're going the extra mile for this girl."

"I do that for all my jobs."

Uncle finished his sandwich, humming with delight. "Yah, right."

Florian was about to protest, but knew in his heart that Uncle John was right. He shook his head and chuckled. "I've only known her a few days. How can I have it so bad?"

"Love is beautiful and mysterious and makes you do crazy things." Uncle John washed his plate.

"What did it make you do?"

"Holly didn't tell you?"

"No. I only know what she gave up."

Uncle John leaned against the other counter and twisted open a green bottle of beer. He pulled out another bottle. "Want one?"

"Sure."

Uncle John twisted the cap off and handed it to him. They clinked bottles and raised them in salute.

"What are we toasting, John?"

"What we sacrifice for love." He took a long pull on the beer.

"I'm not sure I want to sacrifice what Aunt Holly did."

"You'll know soon enough."

"I can't drink to that." Florian eyed his bottle.

"Just drink young man." John shook his head and chuckled.

Florian took a sip of the bitter brew. "Nice."

"You've never tasted Heineken before? You, the foodie in the house?"

"Nope." Never been in love, he realized, either. Not the all-consuming I'll-sacrifice-my-life-as-I-know-it-for-you type love. Is that what was brewing inside of him?

"Uncle John, you were going to tell me what you gave up for Aunt Holly."

"A life of dangerous service." He toasted Florian again with the bottle and took a sip.

Florian sipped and waited for Uncle John to speak.

Finally, Uncle John set his bottle down and rolled it between his hands. "Before I met Holly I was on the fast track for a command post at the station." John worked on the Coast Guard base in Alameda. "But that would have entailed more traveling into—dangerous, more dangerous situations, and I didn't want to do that, to Holly, or me." He stared off into the middle distance. "When push came to shove, I chose Holly over the fast and dangerous track."

"It was 'either-or'?"

"Yes."

"Any regrets?"

"None," Uncle John said without hesitation and raised his bottle to Florian again.

Florian clinked it with his. "Here's to a life with no regrets," he said. That was what he wanted. No regrets. No *what ifs*. No *if onlys*.

He realized he'd lived by those ideas so far, so why stop now? Which meant what exactly? He didn't know, yet. He set his bottle down, having only had one sip, and zipped up his jacket. "I'll go for that walk now."

"No regrets," Uncle John said as he waved Florian out the door.

A vigorous walk up and down San Francisco's steep hills cleared his head. Hours later, he returned to the apartment refreshed and stepped into the shower. He was stepping out when he heard the jingle bells tune on his phone. It was a text from Kate. He'd programmed the ring tone so he'd know a call or text was from her.

She wrote:

Do we have enough magic tricks for the show on Sat?

He dried off, jumped into his pajamas, and slipped under the covers. He chuckled and texted back.

Yep.

His phone jingled with her next text.

You sure?

She followed that with a frowny face emoticon, then a cupcake one, and then a teary face.

She was nervous. Understandable.

He replied:

Double yep.

He followed that up with a smiley face and party hat.

She wrote back:

I THINK WE NEED TO PRACTICE TOMORROW NIGHT.

Florian hesitated before he replied. He'd realized on his long walk up many steep hills that as much as he liked Kate—and he admitted that he liked her a lot—he needed to keep things just friendly, keep his distance. No more staring into hazel eyes. Going home was too important to him. If he stayed, he'd either need to give up his powers, or live in some kind of hiding. His magic would continue to gain in power and instability, since he wasn't channeling it into helping the Pole do its job. He'd be a liability to anyone he tried to help, no longer an asset. He didn't want either of those options. He was going home in nineteen days. He thought he'd feel settled, calmed by his decision. Instead he just felt restless. That must be why he texted back:

SURE. AFTER I TREAT YOU TO A BURGER FOR ALL YOUR HARD WORK.

He added a winky face, a party hat, and a big smiley face.
She texted back right away.

SURE. LIGHT ON THE MAYO.

He laughed and sent back:

LOL

She texted back:

G'NIGHT

He smiled and wrote:

DON'T DREAM OF CUPCAKES.

She sent back a smiley face sticking its tongue out at him.
He laughed again and set the phone down.

Maybe he hadn't made the right choice about keeping his distance.

Chapter Eight

December 4, Thursday

Kate's phone buzzed. Florian was striding away after helping her get set up for the day. Stephanie, her other part time helper, should have been at the cart by now. Her first customers were already lining up for their coffee and cupcakes.

She glanced at the caller ID and answered. "Stephanie, where are you? We're opening."

"I'm sorry, Kate." Stephanie sounded horrible. "I'm sick." She coughed as if to emphasize that fact.

Kate sighed. "I wish you called earlier." Oh no.

"I know. I'm doped on meds and had to set the alarm to call you now."

"Do you think you'll be well for tomorrow?" Fingers crossed.

"I don't think so. I'm so sorry, Kate. It's that darn winter cold going around."

Pressure mounted between her shoulder blades. She rolled her shoulders. There had to be something she could do. "Get better, Stephanie. I hope to see you next week. Things are busy here." She blew out a breath.

"Thanks, Kate. Next week. You're the best." Stephanie coughed again, said goodbye, and hung up.

Kate eyed the line, already five people deep. She hit Florian's number.

He answered cheerily. "Miss me?"

She shook her head and smiled despite the tension lodged behind her shoulder blades. "Hey, can you cover Stephanie's shift?"

"Right now?"

"Yes."

"Be right there."

"Thanks." Some of the tension leaked out of her. "How soon?"

"I'm a few blocks away. I was just about to hop on the bus, so I can be there in five minutes."

"Great." She could manage things until then. She'd worked her cart alone the first few months, in addition to doing all the baking. It wasn't fun. "See you soon. And thanks." Kate clicked the phone off.

He didn't even ask for particulars. Thank goodness she could count on Florian.

Hours later, after a busy day serving customers at the cart, handing off the office orders, and cleaning up with Florian, they headed back to Oakland to unload the van.

"Ready for an early dinner?" Florian stowed the broom in the corner.

"Right, you did promise me a burger. Before we practice for Saturday." She tapped her phone. "I have proof."

"I practice. You watch." He grinned.

I like to watch, she thought but didn't say. A shiver dashed through her and she grinned back.

"Lead the way," Florian said and together they strolled down the busy avenue to Barney's Burgers, only a block away from the kitchen. The restaurant was nearly empty, just a few diners having their late lunches or early dinners. They settled into a corner table by the window, ordered, and sat in companionable silence while the waiter brought them their drinks.

At least Kate felt it was companionable. She hadn't felt this comfortable around a guy in a long time. Relaxed was more like it. She was aware of her business pressure, but felt she could put it aside when she was with Florian. He helped her in such an easeful way. He was really quick and competent in the kitchen, and great with customers. He was a super fast learner and excellent baker. It didn't hurt that he was great to look at. She eyed his lips, and then looked away and sipped her iced tea.

Maybe it was time to include some more fun in her life. Her body tingled all over, as if it had already made up its mind.

With Alex Banks, her ex-boyfriend, there was some kind of pressure to do something, be something, achieve. Maybe because she'd been a college student and the future had felt so uncertain, and because Alex, a graduate student, was already a rising star in his obscure field of mushrooms and other plants in Ancient Greek literature. There'd always been an undercurrent of competition with him that left her feeling that she was always behind in some race.

Now the future was in her hands. She was under a different kind of stress, but at least it was her race, on her terms. Plus, with Florian's help things were starting to look bright. Maybe she could extend the working contract with him into the New Year, if she could convince him to stay.

She leaned forward. "What's your story, Florian?" She sipped her iced tea. "When did you start cooking?"

He smiled and shrugged, then took a sip of his root beer. "Not much to tell, really. I've been a cook and baker for as long as I can remember. My parents joke that I was born with a stirring spoon in one hand and a cookie recipe in the other."

"Cookie?"

"Yah. I was the cookie specialist before I branched out into cakes, pastries, pies, scones, croissants, and now cupcakes."

"Don't forget donuts. Great American pastry."

Florian tapped his spoon on the counter and grinned. "How could I forget about the almighty donut? I've fried them up too."

"And your sister, is she also a baker?"

"My sister?"

"Dahlia, right? She came by the cart yesterday—" Kate nodded her thanks to the waitress who delivered their burgers.

Florian hummed with delight and put his burger together, layering with his long fingers the lettuce, tomato, and pickle. He bit into the four-inch burger and hummed some more.

Kate assembled her burger too and bit into it. Perfect. The medium rare was cooked just how she liked it.

With his burger in one hand, and root beer in the other, he said, "Dahlia's an—um—engineer, an inventor."

"Cool! What does she make?"

"Toys, mostly." Florian glanced away then took a big bite of his burger.

"You come from a creative family. Must be wonderful. You two in such creative fields."

Florian nodded. "It is." He grinned. "How about you?"

Kate shrugged. "We're scholars, teachers, and me, the entrepreneur."

"So you're the black sheep of the family." Florian stated more than asked.

"I guess. My parents are teachers, and Hank, my younger brother—there are just us two kids—you met him the other day, is finishing his bachelor's degree in history at UC Berkeley. He has his sights set on becoming a professor."

"I'm a sort of black sheep, too. My older siblings are all in the toy business. And my younger ones seem set on that track."

"How many of you are there?"

"Ten. Seven brothers and three sisters, including me."

"Kids?"

"Wow. Your parents must really love each other."

"They do." He traced a line on the table, not meeting her gaze. "And I'm part of a triplet. Is that the right way to say it?"

"There are three of you?" Kate chuckled. "Do they all bake as well as you do? I could build my company around your talents."

Florian finished up his burger and shook his head. "No, toy side of things. Basil is into materials and Rowan is a specialist in wheels."

"There must be lots of nuances to the toy industry. Does your family own a manufacturing company?"

"No, well, I guess it's a part ownership. I think you call it a cooperative. I'm not privy to all that, since I went into the kitchens." He shrugged.

"And all of this in Alaska?"

"Just outside Anchorage."

"So outside my world." Kate smiled. "Hey, want to split a chocolate shake for desert?"

"Sure!" He flagged the waitress over and placed their order. "So where did you grow up?"

"In a small town up north, Cloverdale. More cows than people. Good cheese."

"Sounds nice."

"I left as soon as I could."

"Big city. Bright lights." He grinned.

She nodded. "And college."

The waitress delivered the shake with an extra glass, spoon, and straw.

Florian divvied up the shake and handed Kate the spoon and straw and pushed the silver cup to her. "Madame." He nodded ceremoniously.

She took the shake accouterments in hand. "Thank you, sir." Their fingers brushed. Her belly quivered. Yes, she wanted more...of him, of this connection.

He grinned at her, dug in, and took a long draw on the shake. He had a chocolate shake mustache. She giggled and wiped it off.

He curled his upper lip down so she could reach. Then he grinned. "You could be a chocolate shake barber."

"And you could be a comedian." Kate grinned. She felt so at home when she was with him. It had only been four days, but she couldn't see a day go by without him around. She bit back a sigh. She wanted the impossible. He was leaving and she was a workaholic. But maybe things could be different. She could start by not working all the time.

"Do you miss your family?" she asked at the same time he asked, "Why cupcakes?"

"You first," Florian said.

"Cupcakes are fun, petite, and make people smile." Kate slurped her shake.

"Like your boyfriend?"

"What? No boyfriend. Now. I did have one, for a few years, while I was in school. Um, he was an early tester." Kate shrugged and shook her head. "But he's, he's—" She waved her hand in direction of the bay. "We're not together anymore."

Florian eyed her, but said nothing, just watched her spoon her shake.

She let the silence stretch. Alex was in the past. Having a meal with a friend, who also worked for her, that was now, and fun. She didn't have to know about tomorrow, did she? When it came to matters of the heart, Kate realized she was willing to throw caution to the wind and take more chances. It felt good setting down the mantle of responsibility for a little while.

She reached a hand across the table, and Florian took it, squeezing his hand around hers. He smiled at her a little shyly. "I want to know everything about you. I—really like you."

A flush of warmth enveloped her, spreading from her hand held gently, up her arm, and through her whole body. Like champagne, joy bubbled up. "Likewise." She sighed, content as a cat in full purr mode.

He squeezed her hand again and a jolt of electricity shot up her arm. She jumped.

"You okay?" Florian let go of her hand and frowned.

"Static electricity." Kate shook out her hand. "I'm fine. Just startled."

"Sorry about that."

"Not your fault. You must be a good conductor of electricity."

Florian stared off into the distance and sipped his shake. After a moment, he said in a subdued tone, "Your recipes are so fun. What gave you the idea to put pastries into cupcake form?"

"Ah, a topic I can sink my teeth into." She grinned at him, hoping he'd smile back. He seemed a little distant or sad. She wasn't sure.

He didn't smile, but nodded at her, and said nothing, so she continued. "When I was a student at UC Berkeley, I wanted a mini-meal, you know, something small, full of nutrition, especially protein. And I was playing with gluten-free flours, and voila. I'd bring them to class and share them around. My classmates in grad school were my first tasters."

"I thought you said your boyfriend was your first taster."

"Tester, I said. Does sound like 'taster.' " She shrugged. "I met him when I was an undergrad."

"And the cart? What gave you that idea?"

"I didn't want the overhead and lots of employees of a fixed location. I'm an early bird so thought it'd be fun to feed banker and investment types in San Francisco."

"Is it fun?" Florian shoved his empty shake container aside and held out his hands, palm up.

"Sometimes. Most of the time. A lot of the time, now that you're here." She rested her hands in his.

Warmth spread up her arms across her body. She eyed their entwined fingers. It felt so right, even though she knew he was leaving and she'd only have him around for a few more weeks. What was she going to do? I have now, she reminded herself. What if he could stay, another part of her whispered.

"I made things better?"

"Way better." She blew out a breath and dove in. "Any chance you might think about staying on longer...into the New Year?"

"Not everyone is as brilliant as me."

"Humble, not so much? But you didn't answer my question."

Florian chuckled. "Now you know my secret." He blushed.

"Not being humble or not answering my question?" Kate squeezed his hand and disengaged to reach for her purse, immediately missing the warmth that enclosed her when they touched.

"That's mine." He snatched the bill from her. "I invited you."

"Thank you. It's been a while since I've been asked to dinner."

"Why? Your boyfriend—"

"Ex-boyfriend. I told you, he's out of the picture. For over a year."

"What happened?" He asked quietly.

"He left for a professor position at Oxford last summer." She shrugged. "I wanted to stay here and build my business. We went our separate ways."

"Good."

Kate looked at him sideways. "For you or me?"

"For you and me." Florian grinned at her, stood, and held out his hand. "Milady?"

Kate took his hand and let Florian bring her to standing. She wasn't surprised by the sparks that flowed from him into her, she welcomed them, in fact. He still hadn't answered her question.

"Shall we stroll?" He tucked her hand into the crook of his arm, in an old fashioned charming way. They were shoulder to shoulder.

"To the van?" She shivered at their closeness.

"If you like." He gazed into her eyes.

"I like." If her voice sounded husky, she didn't mind.

Florian grinned. She could swear his eyes twinkled but maybe it was the light of the restaurant or of the sky. Dusk was falling. Low sunlight reflected off the fog hovering above them. Kate walked back with him, arm in arm, to her van parked behind the kitchen a block away. There they stood in the cold foggy night.

He smiled down at her. "Still want me to come by to practice the magic show?"

She never really paid attention to their height difference. Maybe because she was a few inches taller in her work shoes and hadn't noticed. Now, she was in her flats and the top of her head came to just above his nose, which had a light dusting of freckles to go with his shock of red, wavy hair.

"Yes, I'd feel better about Saturday." She stared at his lips.

"Did you want to go over the schedule too?"

She nodded and leaned closer to him. "I should."

"But what do you want to do?" he said softly and stepped closer to her.

Somewhere a horn honked. She blinked and gazed into his sparkling green eyes. "I want—" You, I want you to stay, she wanted to say.

He searched her eyes, waiting.

"To have a—" She shook her head. No, she didn't want a fling. But she wanted him, something more meaningful.

He leaned a little closer. "A cupcake nightcap? I know, a wine cupcake."

"I like how you think." She laughed and kissed him on the lips. Just a brief kiss. He was delicious—sweet and alluring.

He leaned in to deepen the kiss, but she pulled away. "Come on. Let's walk to my place. It's not far." She stepped toward the street.

But Florian didn't follow. He chuckled. "You're a bit of a tease."

"I don't mean to be," she said quietly, turned toward him, and held out her hand.

He took her hand. "I know." He cleared his throat. "You keep the van here overnight?"

"It's safe. There are cameras in the lot."

"Will they catch us doing this?" Florian leaned in to land a kiss on her lips. Her insides warmed. She kissed him back. He tasted sweeter than the chocolate shake they'd shared for desert.

She laughed. "I think the cameras have had enough of a show. Let's go."

It took twice as long to walk the fifteen minutes to her apartment. They had to stop every few minutes for more kisses. She felt warm all over, as if she were enveloped in the softest comforter.

They made it up the two flights of stairs without stopping too many times. When she opened the door to her apartment, she felt breathless with the kissing and how he made her laugh with his suggestions for ridiculous cupcake recipes, each one more silly than the next, and jokes about putting on a show for the whole neighborhood.

They stumbled into her front hallway of her one-bedroom apartment. She shut the door behind them and then pulled Florian toward her. "I want to kiss you without walking," she said into his neck. She inhaled his wonderful scent of man and cinnamon. She was burning up and couldn't wriggle out of her coat fast enough. He helped her, and then leaned in for a long, deep kiss that had her sighing and reaching to slip of his coat. She caressed his strong back muscles under his shirt and sighed some more.

When they finally came up for air, he asked, "Don't you want to practice for the party?"

"I want to practice a much more ancient art." She nuzzled his neck and smoothed her hands on his chest, his strong chest, and over his strong muscular arms. He kept himself in good shape. Must be all that lifting and stirring. Too bad he still had his shirt on.

"You sure, Kate?"

"I want you, Florian. I want to be with you." She pulled back to look in his eyes. "I trust you. I know you're ready for the kid's party. I was just stressing out."

He gazed into her eyes. She thought she saw a flicker of doubt or worry, but she couldn't be sure, because then she saw nothing but adoration. He smiled. "I want you, too, Kate. Very much."

She kissed him and pulled him toward her bedroom. "Let's get practicing." She hadn't asked him to stay and he hadn't reminded her he was leaving. At least they had now.

Later that night, she didn't hear the crash coming from the other room, or the bell tone of Florian's phone, lying under the bed, in his pant's pocket. She only heard her joy, and his, and marveled at the glow that surrounded them even though she was sure her eyes were closed in ecstasy.

Chapter Nine

Florian woke up in the middle of the night, for a moment disoriented. Oh, right, he was in Kate's warm bed. Clouds obscured the moon and stars and blanketed the night.

She had one arm flung across his chest, lying on her belly, facing away from him. She was mumbling in her sleep. He couldn't make out the words, but she sounded agitated.

A warm zing flooded him from head to toe. She was wonderful, sweet, but not a pushover, and beautiful with her chestnut hair and eyes that missed nothing. His heart warmed and before he could have a say in it, a bright ball of yellow light, like a mini-sun, burst from his chest and surrounded them, as it had the night before. He wasn't sure. He'd been in a delightfully altered state.

Kate sighed in her sleep and her breathing evened out, her agitation gone.

Something popped and fizzled in the other room. Oh, no. What mess would his magic have him cleaning up? All because he was happy and deeply cared for a woman. He rushed to slip on his jeans, just as his phone rang the school bell tone. He knew it was Aunt Holly without looking at the screen, but he glanced at it anyway. Oh bells. He saw he'd missed an earlier call from her. She must have some kind of super elf magic app that could detect his forbidden use of elf magic. He told Aunt Holly that he couldn't control it, but she hadn't wanted to listen. She only reminded him of what was at stake.

In bare feet, he headed down the hall. He checked the bathroom. Everything looked normal. Next the kitchen. A bottle of soda water on the counter was still bubbling, water dripping across the counter and onto the kitchen floor. His chaotic magic must have caused the top to blow off. He grabbed a sponge by the sink and cleaned up the mess. In his check to be sure he'd caught all the liquid, he noticed a fragment of glass on the far counter. Strange. He opened a cupboard above it and sucked in a breath. Two drinking glasses had shattered, split into mostly big fragments and a few small ones, as small as the shard that had landed on the counter. Dangerous. He looked around for a paper bag to wrap the glasses in. He'd bring them down to the trash personally, and buy two more glasses for Kate. And tell her, what?

He listened to Aunt Holly's voice messages. In the first, she said was, "What is going on? Hope you're okay. Remember the cost. And, have a—good time." and then in the second message, all she said was, "Florian, I'm concerned."

He texted her back.

I'M FINE. NO ONE WAS AFFECTED OR SAW.

He knew the cost. But for the first time, he realized that he was considering giving it all up for Kate—the wonderful job in his community that he loved, full of amazing and creative elf siblings, parents, cousins, aunts and uncles. To not go back? To lose his magic? Did he really want to pay such an expensive amount to be with Kate? She was wonderful, but he barely knew her. Yet, he knew her enough to know he really liked her. His crazy magic was proof of his joy at being around her. He needed to sleep on it. He yawned, slipped into Kate's cozy small living room and plunked into the easy chair. He grabbed a convenient blanket off the back of the love seat and wrapped himself up to let some soothing dreams find him.

Kate found him in her living room, asleep, legs pulled up to his chest. Her heart fluttered. She smiled. Flexible guy. She'd experienced just how flexible last night. She smoothed her palm over his morning stubble and kissed his cheek.

Florian smiled and, eyes still closed, circled his arms around Kate and pulled her in for a kiss on the lips. "Hey you, good morning."

Kate hummed into the kiss. When she came up for air, she said, "It is a good morning. Bed not comfortable enough for you?"

He opened his eyes and glanced away. "Uh. I got a call from the family. Didn't want to disturb."

"Everything okay?" She headed toward the bathroom.

After a moment, he said. "Yah."

She paused at the doorway. "I'm jumping in the shower. I want to leave for the kitchen in thirty minutes."

"Want company?" he smirked at her.

"No." She sighed and smiled, giving him a sidelong glance. "We'll never get to the kitchen in time. We have extra batches to make, remember?"

"I do. Want me to make coffee?" He stood and stretched, his belly showing as his t-shirt rode up.

She stared, and then glanced away. "Yes, but the espresso machine is at the kitchen. On purpose." She called over her shoulder. "But you can make me an egg with steamed kale."

"Yes, ma'am. Kale! Coming right up."

She laughed, shut the bathroom door, and turned on the shower. She could get used to this. She wanted to get used to this. All she had to do was ask him to stay with her and with her company. They made a great team. Her heart pounded in her chest. She wanted this, badly. He was wonderful. Sexy, sweet, kind, and funny. Oh and a great baker. How hard could it be to ask him? He hadn't said anything, so she had to make the first move.

Fifteen minutes later, she was dressed and sitting in front of a sunny side up egg and steamed kale at her kitchen counter. Just the way she liked it. The whole package. She gazed up at him and blinked at the tear leaking from her eye.

"You're a keeper." She rose up on the stool enough to reach him and plant a kiss on his lips.

He returned her kiss with a broad smile and strode to the bathroom. In a minute, the shower was running. She realized she hadn't asked him what he wanted for breakfast. A plate and fork was already washed and perched in her dish rack. He'd fed himself. What was his favorite kind of morning eggs? She wanted to know.

She wolfed down the delicious breakfast and pulled her planner out of her bag. She flipped to the back where she kept plans for expansion. She'd been looking for the right business partner, not wanting to rush into anything too soon. She'd heard horror stories from her colleagues about bad partnerships and investors ruining businesses almost before they even got off the ground. That was why she'd taken her time, not wanting to jump into investor or business partner relationships. But maybe with the right offer, Florian would stay. She reread her plans and made some notes.

Twenty minutes later, they were at the kitchen at the early hour of 4 a.m. Florian appreciated the brisk walk in the early morning fog from Kate's apartment to the kitchen. The neighborhood was quiet, except for a few really early Friday drivers and pre-dawn joggers.

Florian liked the sly smile on Kate's lips as she sipped the cappuccino he made for her. He liked cooking for her. He liked baking with her. In fact, he liked everything about her, including how driven she was. And he especially liked how content he felt. He didn't have the urge to move on to the next location. What if he stayed? His heart fluttered, a butterfly wanting to fly free. The restless spirit that had pushed him from place to place throughout the year to learn in new places with new people seemed to have faded in the background. Even with the intense schedule working with Kate, he had enough variety to keep him satisfied. And that had a lot to do with Kate.

Then his heart squeezed. His next location was home. Where his boisterous family was, his serious triplet brothers, more sisters than he could manage, a kitchen fixed up to perfection, Uncle with his discerning and impeccable taste, always happy to see him, and demanding for the next new tastes. He'd get his Master Baker badge and cap and be in charge of his own kitchen, and no longer be an apprentice under others. There were a lot of mouths to feed and bodies to keep happy at the Pole. A job he could be proud of. Lots of new recipes to impress everyone with what he'd learned in the last year.

And Kate didn't know. Didn't know who he really was, what he truly wanted in life. He sucked in a breath. It'd been easy to keep his identity a secret this past year, but now it didn't feel so easy. He wanted to open up to her, in every way. Yet, if he did... he'd lose all he'd worked so hard for.

She'd glanced at him when he'd sucked in a breath, but he could see her attention was on other things. She sipped the cappuccino he made her, gave a little sigh of contentment, bent to scribble more notes in her planner.

He finished cleaning up from making them coffee and got to work on the first batch of cupcakes: today's lunch special turkey and mozzarella. He couldn't tell her who he really was. He really did want to go home again and step into his new position of responsibility. But he didn't regret last night, and he loved working side by side with her. She was a pro at her business, a hard worker, sweet, gorgeous, and so creative.

Kate soon joined him and together they worked in a nice rhythm to get all the cupcakes prepped for the day and for the special office orders.

As they loaded the van, two hours later, Kate said, "I have a project idea I wanted to bounce off you. Can you take a look at it while we head to the City?"

"Sure." He smiled. "I like having things bounced off me."

She laughed and blushed. They got into the van, and she handed him some sheets of paper from her planner, she'd tugged out of their binder rings.

"You tore pages out of your planner? I thought that thing was like your bible."

She smiled, revved the engine, and navigated them toward the freeway. "It is, but I can put those back."

Florian nodded and eyed the top sheet. Written across the top in her neat script handwriting were the words, "Expansion 2.0."

"Your expansion plans."

"Tell me what you think." She kept her eyes on the rode.

"Just like that? What are your criteria for success?" He scanned her extensive notes.

"Just read, will you?" She glanced at him, concern in her gaze.

"Sure." So while Kate barreled down the freeway toward the Bay Bridge, Florian read her notes. She wanted to add lunch delivery and home delivery using bike messengers and car services. Nice. Plus more themed parties throughout the year.

"Based on what you have here, you'll need a full time baker. Probably two. And some working capital probably for extra party help. You can't work all the time," he said when he finished flipping through her expenses and income projections. "It could work."

"With the right people," Kate said, without glancing at him.

There was light traffic and they were already on the western span of the Bay Bridge. The city, cloaked in fog, winked awake as the work day began.

"With the right people, it could be really fun."

"And a lot of work."

"And fun." Florian glanced at her.

"Yes." Kate smiled and glanced back. She said nothing more as she drove into downtown and parked beside their spot. She turned off the engine and looked at him. She waved to the pages he was still holding. She blew out a breath, glanced out the window, and then squared her body to face his. "Florian, would you like to join my expansion team? We haven't really talked about next year. And—" She searched his eyes for something, then barreled forward. "I'd really like to have you on my team in the New Year. After a vacation, of course. Well earned. For both of us."

He opened his mouth, and then closed it again. He should have seen her request coming. "Kate, I—" He set her planner pages on the dash and took her hands in his. He gazed at her, trying to convey all he felt. The deep adoration he had for her, the need to go home, his desire for her—all real, all stirring together within him. "I wish I could."

"I just thought we make a great team—here and—" She waved at the van and between them.

"We do." He squeezed her hands, trying to reassure her. "I'm here for a few more weeks and can help you get things ready for next year." And I really, really like you, he thought but didn't say.

"I know we made no promises last night." Kate blinked back a tear and lifted her chin. "And I love being in the now with you."

"Being in the now?"

She tugged her hands away from his and stared out the window. "Never mind. It was a stupid idea. Let's just get to work." She jumped out of the van. He heard the back doors open. He jumped out to join her in unpacking. He guarded the wares while she went to get the cart without another word to him. He wanted to reach out to her, smooth away her worry lines on her forehead, kiss away her frown. He wanted to hug her and whisper that it was all going to work out. His heart sank. He liked her, a lot. But was that enough to give up his Master Baker position back home?

Chapter Ten

December 5

In the hour after presenting her dumb proposal to Florian, Kate had set up the cart, with Florian's very capable help, and opened shop, all with saying the bare minimum to him. She still didn't know what to say to him as the first morning rush slowed to a trickle. It had been a dumb idea. She hadn't felt at all awkward waking up with him in her apartment this morning, but now she was not sure where they stood.

Into the beeping of car horns and a distant foghorn blaring, Florian said, as if picking up on her thoughts, "Kate, it's not a dumb idea."

Kate brushed her hair back into its bun and dried her hands on a dishtowel to stall for time. How did he always seem to know what she was dwelling on?

Florian straightened items on the small counter, removing and replacing them as he wiped down the counters, thorough, diligent—she never had to ask him to keep on top of things in the kitchen because he always did.

He glanced up at her and paused in his movements when she didn't answer right away.

She glanced away. Pedestrians strode down the sidewalk, intent on wherever they were going, whatever they were doing. She had intent and focus, but didn't want to be alone in her endeavors anymore. Even now, she wanted to lean into his willowy strength. A partner, he could be a partner in her business and maybe in her life. The strong and sudden yearning hurt in her chest, it was so strong.

"I don't know if I can do this." She gestured between them and let herself look into his eyes. "I mean—"

"Are you firing me?" He spoke quietly and kept his gaze level with hers, his look hurt but also curious, and kind.

"No. Of course not." Kate shook her head and blew out a breath. "I—just—I don't know. You've done nothing wrong. We've done nothing wrong. We're two consenting adults. I was just hoping—it was foolish to hope." To want you in my life. She scrubbed both hands across her face and turned to straighten the trays on the shelf for the lunch orders that didn't need straightening.

"Kate." He called softly.

She blinked back the unruly tears, squared her shoulder, and turned to face him.

"Kate, we're good together. In the kitchen and—" He dried his hands and folded the cloth neatly. "Come here." He held out a hand to her.

"But for how long?" she whispered.

Just then a customer approached the window. Florian pressed a hand on her arm and stepped to the window to take the order. He popped the croissant cupcake into the oven to heat and busied himself at the espresso machine to make a latte.

A heavy silence hovered between them. "Florian, never mind. We don't owe—I'm just—I can see that I was dreaming." She grabbed her coat and stepped out of the cart. "I'll be back in fifteen." She didn't wait to see his response. He could handle the cart and the customers.

She didn't know if she could handle herself.

When had she fallen for Florian? When had she built castles in the sky around him and a possible future together? She strode down to Market Street, turned left at the Ferry Building and strode past tourists. She shoved her hands into her coat pockets, not really seeing the wheeling seagulls, picking off tourist scraps. The northern-western wind blew down on her. She had to fight against it to progress up the Embarcadero.

She knew when. It was when she woke up this morning and discovered Florian curled up in her easy chair. Instead of feeling upset that he left the bed, she was appreciative that he felt so comfortable in her home. It was when he greeted her so warmly and when he made her breakfast. It was how he treated her, all the time, and especially the morning after. She felt excited and inspired. She felt at home, and at peace. She didn't need to worry. Things would work out. She could relax and just enjoy her life. She couldn't remember the last time she felt that way.

By the time she sorted all that out, she'd already strode down to Pier 23, and could see a cruise ship docked at Pier 27. She searched her pockets for her smart phone to check the time and swore. She'd left it back at the cart, and she was pretty sure she'd been gone already at least fifteen minutes. And she wasn't any closer to a solution. Of course, she didn't want to fire Florian, and she couldn't stop seeing him, at least professionally. He was wrapped up in all levels of her business. And in her heart.

She'd just have to not have him over at her place. Clearly, that would only end with them in bed and him embedded more deeply into her heart. She had to let that dream go. She hadn't realized how much she wanted a heart and business partner. She hadn't realized how all consuming her business had become, or how much she'd let it devour all her energy, with no room for fun.

Florian invited fun, play, joy. She wanted more of that in her life. Maybe later, maybe with another, like him. Right now, she needed to get back to the cart. And Florian. She wanted Florian. Another fifteen minutes later, she was back at the cart, and the early lunch rush was in full swing.

"You okay?" Florian asked, over the noise of the espresso machine, worry in his gaze.

She nodded, sloughed off her coat, hung it up, and tied on her apron. "Need a break?"

"I'm good. Where do you want me?" He handed the customer her coffee and cupcake and made change.

"The window is fine." Kate placed herself between the espresso machine and the trays of cupcakes.

Florian nodded and started calling out orders to her.

In the next lull, thirty minutes later, Florian finished his cleaning up and then turned to her. "Come here, Kate." He held out his hands to her.

She shook her head and glanced away. "I need to not do that."

He dropped his hands and stuck them into his jeans pocket. "Talk to me then. I can help you."

"That's the thing. You are helping me. Have been helping me." She gestured to the cart, and then rubbed her shoulders. "It's just that—we can't do this personal thing, between us." She gulped and busied herself with cleaning the counter.

"I know. It was a mistake." Florian said.

"No, it wasn't." Kate felt her face flame. "How could you say that?"

"No, that's not what I meant. Kate!" He reached out to her, but she didn't reach back. "No, I—it's just that I have other obligations." He shook his head and grabbed his coat. "I need to make a call." He stepped out of the cart before she could say anything.

Kate rolled her aching shoulders. Thankfully, a customer stepped up to the window.

Business and love just didn't mix. Never had in her life.

Why did she think this time things would be different?

Chapter Eleven

A few hours later, Florian checked the kitchen. It was clean, ready for tomorrow's party prep. They were back in Oakland. Business had been brisk, with people chatty and telling him all kinds of wonderful stories. Bells. It was happening again. His magic was seeping into his food. So far all the stories were wonderful, like how a long-lost friend had contacted them, or their son had been especially happy that morning, or their sweetheart had made them her favorite dinner. In the past, he'd left before things got too—he didn't know what. He'd always left a previous job before things escalated. But he felt like they would, so it was just one more reason to go to the next gig.

Florian was in a pickle. He smiled wryly at that analogy. He just hoped the consequences of eating his food—a side effect no elf had ever talked to him about—remained positive. His aunt hadn't mentioned it; his sister hadn't. And they weren't allowed to contact home, so there was no way to check from that quarter. He checked the supplies closet.

"You'll need more gluten-free flour soon and chocolate chips."

Kate was making notes in her planner. "Hmmm" came her non-committal answer. She'd been giving him one-word non-answers for the last few hours.

He couldn't blame her. She was keeping her distance. He understood.

But it hurt. He couldn't expect any more. Now that their relationship had progressed fast beyond a working relationship to a personal one. He took off his apron and folded it. He placed it on the counter near Kate, but she didn't look up from her work.

He strode to the door, and then turned to face her. "I'll see you at your brother's party tonight?"

Kate popped her head up, eyes wide. "Darn. I forgot all about that." She focused on him, sadness in her gaze.

He wanted to comfort her, hated seeing her sad. But he stayed frozen by the door to the parking lot and waited for her reply.

"You're going back to the city, then returning to Berkeley for the party?"

"I'm not sure." He shrugged. "I think I'll go exploring. If I walk north I'll hit Berkeley, right?"

Kate nodded and rolled her shoulders. "College Avenue runs right into campus in about a mile and a half."

"Sounds about right." He nodded.

"Right for what?" Her curiosity was peaked. She'd set down her pen.

"Mentally rehearse tomorrow's show and solve all the world's cookie problems."

"The world has cookie problems?"

"Yes, and a cupcake problem, but that one's harder."

"There's not enough of them?" A whisper of a smile on Kate's face made him happy.

"See? You see the problem too." He smiled.

Did he really want to walk away from her and go back home?

She picked up the pen and tapped it on the other hand. "I guess we can talk about that at the party tonight."

Hope bubbled in his chest, as if he were schoolboy with his first crush. She was talking to him and wanted to continue to do so.

"Good." He nodded again, trying not to grin. He wanted to swoop her up in his arms and kiss her silly.

"Have a good walk, Florian. See you soon." She stilled her pen tapping and turned back to her planner. "Sorry about—" She waved around at the kitchen, encompassing them, and all her delicious innovative recipes that had found a way to his heart.

"No need." He waved at her. "Bye." He abruptly turned and stepped out, unable to meet her eye. What had he just said no to?

He walked briskly for a time up the street, not noticing people, and cars, except to make sure he crossed the street at the right moments.

After a time, he shook his head and huffed. The cool cloudy afternoon, with the smell of rain in the air, was the first thing he noticed besides that he was walking in the right direction. His mixed-up emotions jumbled in his heart. On the one hand, he wanted to be with Kate. On the other, he wanted to take his place at home. But all he could do right now was walk to

Berkeley and check out the sights. Maybe by the time he got to Berkeley, he'd have an answer to what he really wanted.

But thirty minutes later, a decaf espresso in hand, and clear view of the UC Berkeley campus across the street from the near-empty patio at Cafe Roma, he still had no such answer.

If he went home, and took his place as Master Baker of Deserts, a place he'd been working toward for years, he'd have professional satisfaction and personal satisfaction, too. He'd eventually marry. Elves lived a long time, especially those who stayed at the Pole. The middle McDougal girl was nice. They could maybe make a go of it one day. No champagne bubbles popped in his chest when he thought of the middle McDougal girl.

Or, he could declare his love for Kate, and tell her his secret, and give up his elf life, for her, and a life they could cook up together, for however long she'd take him—because it might not work out. It's not like they'd declared for each other. He was grinning into his espresso cup. His heart pounded in his ears, like bubbles popping at a New Year's party.

And yet, and yet... That was an awful lot to give up based on a relationship that had just begun. And though he'd been working closely with Kate for five days, really liked her, maybe they weren't meant to be. How could he know?

She'd thought they had a future together when she'd asked him to be a part of her business. After they slept together. She did want him in her life.

Had he ruined his chances by turning her down?

He needed more information about Kate.

He picked up his phone and dialed.

"Hello?"

"Hey, Hank, this is Florian, Kate's baker. You invited me to your party tonight."

"I remember! Hey, you still coming I hope!"

"In fact, I'm in Berkeley now and—"

"Cool, come on by. We're just getting set up now. You can hang out."

"Or help."

"Yah, sure. Whatever." Hank laughed. "I'm sure you're all tuckered out. I know my sister works her employees hard."

Florian chuckled. "Good thing I'm not an employee."

"You're not? You working for free?"

"No, I'm a contractor."

"Wow, she must really like you to deviate from her well-thought out plans."

"Yah, well—" Florian shrugged and maybe he sighed too because Hank exclaimed, "What? You and her!"

Florian shook his head. "I'll explain when I get there."

"I don't believe it. My straight-laced sister breaking her own rules for—"

"I'll see you soon, Hank." Florian hung up before he could hear Hank's characterization of who he must be.

Florian wanted to be face-to-face with Kate's brother to work out what felt more delicate than a soufflé cupcake. He followed the map directions to the fraternity house, just above the university campus. A decorative sculpture arrangement ringed a fountain on the front garden. He stepped up to the front door and knocked.

A man about thirty answered the door. "Can I help you?" he said in a French accent.

Florian was taken aback for a moment, expecting to see a college student answering the door. "Uh, yes, I'm here a bit early, for the party."

The man nodded. "Yes, we are preparing for the festivities, but weren't expecting guests at this hour." The man didn't budge, but guarded the open space between the open door and the jamb.

"I'm here to see Hank. He's expecting me."

Florian heard a voice call out. "Let him in, Julien. He's good people. I'll vouch for him."

"You'd better," Florian heard the man called Julien say under his breath, as Julien stepped back to let him in, frowning.

Florian nodded. "Thank you, sir." He didn't want to get the bouncer or guard, or whatever Julien was, angry.

Hank strode toward through a big living room area toward him and held out his hand. "Florian, my man."

When Florian grasped it, Hank pulled him into a quick hug and slapped him on the back. "Don't mind, Julien. He's just looking out for us. He's a really great guy. He's our new— mentor. I think that's the right word to describe him. Anyway, let me introduce you to him. Then you can hang with us while we get things set up around here."

Florian shook hands with Julien, a tall broad-shouldered man who looked like he worked outdoors with his sun-brown complexion. There was a look in his eye, as if he'd travelled far and wide. He'd seen that look before in his travels. There was something else about Julien—his accent maybe. It was French-sounding, but like nothing he'd heard before.

Julien nodded his greeting. "You are a visitor to these parts, I have heard. I too don't originate from here."

"France, yes?" Florian asked. The man had a strong grip.

"Indeed." Julien gave him the once over, as if evaluating him, and still deciding if he measured up.

Florian, usually not at a loss for words, couldn't think of anything to say, funny or otherwise.

Julien nodded again. "There is something different about you, Florian McMillian." He squinted, gave Florian the once over again, quickly, and then nodded as if he'd decided Florian's measure. "You have been near the Northern Lights."

"I've seen the Aurora Borealis. I'm from Alaska," Florian said, nervous butterflies jumping in his chest.

"Not those lights," Julien said.

Florian said nothing. He'd never had anyone even guess or hint at his true identity since he'd been on his year abroad in the States.

"Why do you say that, Julien?" Hank said and shoved a cushion chair against the wall, straightening the sitting room that was clean and clear of clutter.

That was when Florian spotted the huge portrait painting hung above the fireplace mantle. He shivered at the uncanny resemblance to the man in front of him—Julien—the one who was looking at him oddly, with too much of a knowing gaze. Florian shifted from foot to foot.

Julien glanced at the painting behind him and gestured with his chin. "My ancestor, we believe."

Hank tossed a pillow from one end of the couch to the other and said with pride in his voice, "That's Flavius Aetius, the founder of our fraternity, as the legend goes. He was the last great general of the Western Roman Empire, born 391, dies 454, a few years after the major and decisive battle against the

Huns. He was commonly known as Aetius. Julien looks just like him. Isn't that cool? Julien is also our resident artist. He's a sculptor, not a paint—"

"Stone mason, Hank." Julien interrupted and gave Hank a stern look.

"Sorry, stone mason," Hank said to Julien. He turned to Florian. "Didn't mean to give you a history lecture." He shrugged apologetically and continued his pillow rearranging.

Julien turned his gaze back to Florian. "I too have seen the Northern Lights. A version of them, perhaps." For a moment, his gaze turned inward. Then he clamped a strong hand on Florian's shoulder. "Wherever you are from, I welcome you to Psi Alpha Omega Chi house."

"Thanks, Julien." Florian nodded. He liked this serious man who saw more than others but wasn't going to blabber about it, or be too nosy.

Hank tugged at the big couch, but it didn't budge much. Florian then Julien pushed and pulled it into place, so there was more open space in front of the huge fireplace.

Hank surveyed the room. "Looks good. Let's deal with the kitchen." He eyed Florian. "But not you, dude. You've probably had your fill of kitchens for the week."

Florian shrugged. "Dude, I'm a baker. Kitchens are my second home. Like—"

"Like libraries are for me. Since I'm a student." Hank grinned.

"Exactly!" Florian slapped him on the shoulder. "Besides I need to have a serious conversation with you. And kitchens are were I'm used to having them."

Hank nodded knowingly and touched his nose. "Let's go then."

"I'll man the front," Julien said.

"Thanks, Julien." Hank said soberly.

Florian followed Hank into a big kitchen, set up in a wide U shape. Counters formed the arms of the U and were covered in sodas, bags of many kinds of chips, paper cups, plates, napkins, all still in their plastic wrappings.

"Want something?" Hank waved over the offerings.

"No, I'm good."

Hank nodded and then yelled out. "Guys, let's get going."

A tromping of shoes on stairs and hardwood floors and soon the kitchen was full of guys saying Hi to him and setting up for the party.

Hank poured himself a cup of soda and motioned for Florian to follow him. They walked down the hall and into a billiards room. Hank took a sip of his drink, set it down, then gathered up the cups and plates scattered about the tall bar tables ringing the walls.

"Just a sec," Hank said. "I thought the guys took care of this room already." He shook his head and carried the items out.

He was back in a moment. "So what's up with you and my sister?" He motioned for Florian to sit with him on a tall stool at one of the cocktail tables.

Florian wished he had something in his hands. "Do you have any beer around here?"

Hank shook his head. "We're a dry fraternity."

"Dry?"

"No alcohol."

"Oh. Maybe I'll go for that soda after all. You guys have root beer?"

"Sure. Ice?"

"Nah."

"Be right back." Hank slapped him on the back and chuckled, but was kind enough to withhold his comments.

He was back with a paper cup and a liter bottle of A&W Root Beer. He set them in front of Florian. "It's not the fancy stuff. Hope you don't mind."

"Root beer-flavored sugar water is pretty much the same worldwide." Florian grinned and sipped.

"Spill it." Hank said and sat on the stool across from him.

The room was dim. Night had fallen. Florian gazed at Hank. "I'm not sure where to begin."

Hank nodded, but said nothing.

"Kate asked me to work with her next year in her business expansion plans. They're really good, but—"

"She must really like you to ask you that. And trusts you. And like you." Hank grinned at his repetition, clearly enjoying himself.

"I really like her, too. She's wonderful. And such a fun business."

"What did you tell her?"

"That I had another commitment."

"Is that true?"

"Of course. But I was surprised by her offer and want to seriously consider it."

"It's more than business, though."

He sipped his root beer. "It's a big deal."

"It is." Hank squeezed his cup, peered inside it, and poured himself some root beer.

"You know Kate well, being her brother and all. Is she—? I mean, how is she with—?" Florian threw his hands in the air. "I don't know exactly what I'm asking."

"You want to know if she's worth it."

Florian shook his head and smiled into his drink, staring at the bubbles. "No, she's definitely worth it."

"And she obviously thinks you are, too, otherwise she wouldn't have presented the offer to you."

Florian nodded and said quietly, "But—what if it doesn't work out? I can't go back to my other commitment. That ship will have sailed." He stared at his half-filled cup of root beer, not really seeing it, and shifted on the stool.

Hank shook his head then shrugged. "I don't have any personal experience to draw on. But my sister, she's good people. If you're sure, and she's sure, I say, 'go for it.' Not that you need me to give you permission, dude, come on. This is the twenty-first century."

Florian cracked a smile and shrugged. "I know. We do things a little differently where I come from. So thank you for your blessing. That helps."

"You want to go talk to my dad? We could call him. He's probably reading at this hour."

Florian sipped his drink, considering seriously. "No, I don't think that will be necessary. I don't—I'm not sure what I want."

"Really!" Hank slapped Florian playfully on the shoulder. "Did you find out what you wanted to about my hard-headed, stubborn, gutsy, risk-taking brilliant sister?"

"You forgot to add excellent cook and beautiful, too."

"We come from good, hardy stock."

Florian laughed. "My people too."

"You're from Alaska, right. That's far."

Florian chuckled. "Yep. You haven't traveled much?"

"No." Hank shook his head and then shrugged. "I couldn't afford to do the year abroad. But hopefully for grad school I'll travel at some point. Italy, man! France too!"

"They're wonderful." Florian sipped his root beer.

"What are the Northern Lights like?"

Florian gazed out the window to the night. "Beautiful. Like nothing you've ever seen. Dancing shimmering rainbows at night."

Hank sighed and gulped down his drink. "One day, I'll see them." He slapped the table with his cup. "Well, I got to oversee the troops. Make sure we're ready for the party that starts in—" He glanced at his smart phone.

A chime sounded.

"Now!"

Florian chuckled and stood, gulping down his drink, a little too fast. Bubbles went up his nose. He coughed and managed to say, "Need any help?"

"Nah, you get to chill and mingle with the guests." Hank headed out of the room. Florian followed him into the large living room. He still hadn't decided what to do: stay for Kate and their burgeoning relationship or go home. He sneezed at the bubbles still lingering in his nose.

People were streaming into the fraternity house. He nodded hello and then, there she was, all dressed up in a burgundy red dress that hugged her curves in all the right places and brought out the red in her chestnut hair striped with that fun green. His heart pounded. The bubbles in his whole body danced.

He couldn't leave her. He'd declare his heart and tell her the truth tonight—here. A wave of joy swept through him, blinding him for a moment, so he faltered in his step toward Kate to greet her. A man intercepted her before he could. This man was about as tall as he was, but with broad shoulders, wavy dark brown hair, and when he turned slightly to kiss Kate on the cheek, Florian caught a glimpse of his chiseled face, a prominent dimple in his chin.

Kate smiled at the man and threw her arms around his neck. She said something, but Florian couldn't hear it over the noise of the room, or over the roaring in his ears. All the bubbles popped. Instead of feeling deflated like a flat balloon, he felt fueled. He strode over to Kate and the mysterious man, not noticing the people who quickly cleared from his path.

"Florian," Kate said brightly. "So good to see you here." She kissed him on the cheek. "This is Alex Banks, my—"

"Former boyfriend," Alex said in a clipped British accent.

Handsome, strong, and a suave British accent.

"Alex, this is Florian McMillian, my—"

"Her baker." Florian held out his hand and gripped Alex's.

Alex had a strong grip, but he could hold his own. He wielded sharp utensils for a living.

"Kate, can I get you something to drink?" Florian asked, turning his back on Alex.

"I can get it myself." Kate looked between the two of them. "Actually, Florian, can I talk to you for a minute?" She looked at Alex. "Baking stuff. For tomorrow."

Alex nodded graciously.

She slipped her hand through Florian's arm and whispered to him. "I need to—"

"I have to talk to you," Florian said at the same time.

"What?" Kate looked at him, her gaze level to his.

She must be wearing heels.

"I know I don't have any claim on you, Kate, but—"

"Wait, Florian. I was stupid. I shouldn't have given you the cold shoulder all afternoon."

"You were pissed."

"No, I was disappointed. I shouldn't have expected you to—" She stepped closer to him. They were in the busy hallway between the living area and the kitchen.

Florian put a hand on her waist and pulled her closer. "It's okay. It's all okay." And leaned in to kiss her. She was his.

"Get a room," someone shouted.

Laughter.

Kate chuckled. "Want to?"

"I so do. But we need to talk first," Florian said. "Is there a place where we can do that were we won't be spied upon by loud college students?"

Kate nodded and grabbed his hand. "Mind going for a little walk? It's a bit cold."

"Not as cold as where I come from."

But he may never see as an insider ever again once he told Kate who he really was, and showed her too. Would she accept him as he really was?

Chapter Twelve

In the cool evening, Florian strolled with Kate down a small street, turning left, then right, and a few more turns until they arrived at the college campus. Hands clasped and swinging, he followed where she led, into new territory.

The evening was quiet, not many students out at the dinner hour. A tall clock tower as their apparent beacon, Kate led them deeper into the trails and tiny forests nestled between massive stone buildings until they arrived at steps leading directly to the tall clock tower.

She squeezed his hand, sighed, and led him up steps to the base of the tower. She turned them so that the clock tower was at their backs. Without a word, she stopped, a half smile gracing her kissable lips. He leaned toward her. She shook her head and gestured ahead of them.

"Oh!" How could he not have seen the view? He only had eyes for her. Peering through the fog, the Golden Gate twinkled in the far distance, like a necklace across the neck of the bay. "Very nice."

"You haven't seen the best part," Kate said softly.

He glanced at her. This time he did lean in and, turning his back on the marvel of the bridge in the distance, he kissed the marvel right in front of him. He put all his emotion into the kiss—his love for her, the import of what he was about to do— how was he going to tell her? He broke off the kiss and glanced up at the clock tower. "Does it play?"

Kate turned, following his gaze. "The Campanile chimes on the hour. Pretty sure someone plays the bells during the day. At least they did when I was a student."

"I'd love to hear them play. I love bells of all kinds," Florian said and wrapped his arms around her. He knew what he could do to show her who he really was. Actions spoke louder than words.

Kate slipped her phone out of her coat pocket. "If they're going to ring, they should in about fifteen minutes." She gazed at him and smoothed his stubble on his cheek.

He leaned toward her for another delicious kiss, but she turned her head so the kiss landed on her cheek and said, "What did you want to talk to me about?"

Florian pulled back and gazed into her hazel eyes that looked green in the lamplight. "Your offer took me by surprise." He smiled and shook his head.

"A little too fast? Sorry about that."

"Maybe a little." He chuckled. "Don't be sorry. Never be sorry for what we have. Besides, I'm the one who needs to be sorry."

"What do you mean? I seduced you with wine." She hugged him against her, so their bodies fit together. Even with their coats in the way, heat rolled off her.

"You did, did you?" Florian stole a kiss.

Kate kissed him back and the kiss flared. After a few intense heated moments, she pulled back, breathing fast, and smiled. "I am kind of pushy."

"Only in the best way. You know what you want. I like that in a woman."

"Oh?"

"And I know how to hold my own," Florian whispered and kissed her neck. Her scent of lilac, cinnamon, and woman enveloped him. Maybe he'd been taken in by the unique magic of Kate. He had to tell her. Now.

"Hmmm." She hummed. "You can handle it, the business, me," Kate said softly. "That's why I made the offer."

"I can handle you, Kate." He gripped her waist under her coat.

She slipped her hands under his coat and caressed his back. "I'm a lot to handle. I like to take charge, be bossy. I'm stubborn, and mercurial."

"Is this a sales pitch?" Florian eyed her lips. "You don't need to sell me on you, Kate. I am already sold."

"You are?" Kate's eyes widened, and then she squeezed him in a tight hug. "Does this mean you'll stay—with me—the business—all of it?"

"All of it, Kate. Yes." He squeezed his eyes shut at the bubble of joy that exploded in his chest. Heat enveloped him. "But there's something you should know."

She released him from the hug and blinked, leaving a wave of cold air in her stead. Had she seen the golden aura that surrounded them? She said nothing, just shoved her hands in her pockets, and lifted her chin. "Am I going to like what I hear?"

He chuckled. "It's not as if I have a deep dark secret."

She gazed at him, without a smile, her serious I-mean-business face on.

He wanted to reach out to her. Telling her straight out was harder than he ever imagined. He hadn't really rehearsed it though. He blew out a breath. "Well, I'm not all that I seem." In the lamplight, Florian searched her eyes for a sign of softness. She appeared in neutral, ready to surf with whatever wave would come her way. Brave woman. That was one of the things he loved about her. He puffed out a breath. "What I'm about to tell you will change everything."

She nodded and held his gaze. "For you and me?"

Florian nodded and gulped. He was stalling, he knew. Here goes. "It's better if I show you." He waved his hand. For a moment nothing happened. Then the campanile bells chimed a melodic Celtic riff. A shimmer of sparkles flew from his fingertips into the air arcing like a rainbow toward the bells at the top of the tower.

She gasped. "Did you do that?"

"You can see it?" He asked just as his cell phone rang with the school bell tones. He ignored the phone. He didn't care anymore about his aunt's warnings. His magic didn't harm anyone. It brought beauty, and for however long he still had it, he wanted to share the beauty.

She nodded, her mouth open a little, and stared up at the sparkles fading into the night.

A few lamps on the Campanile esplanade popped and fizzled out, throwing sparks to the ground. One of the sparks landed next to Kate. He rushed to stomp it out, his heart beating too fast. That wasn't supposed to happen. The bells quieted.

She turned to him, her hands still in her coat pockets. "I don't understand. You didn't answer. That was you making the bells ring and the lamps blow out?"

He stared at the black smudge on the stone and glanced back at her. "The world is full of more mysterious and magical things than we can imagine." He gulped. His heart pounded fast, as if it were a trapped animal. His phone buzzed again. What? He grimaced when he looked at the caller ID and shut off the ring again.

"Do you need to get that?" she said.

He shook his head and gazed at her. Her eyes had shifted and seemed chocolate brown now. He opened his mouth and then snapped it shut.

"What's going on, Florian? Are you okay? What was that?" She waved at the tower. "Some magic trick?"

"No." He shoved his hands into his pocket. "Maybe we should head back."

She tilted her head at him. "I thought you were going to tell me something." Then she shook her head. "We can go back."

Florian wanted to reach for Kate's hands to warm them up, but he felt frozen. If he told her, that was it. There was no going back. Maybe their relationship was too fragile for this step. Maybe he should wait. He didn't want to think of himself as a chicken in the matters of the heart, but maybe he was. Maybe he was being smart and not putting so much pressure on whatever was blossoming between him and Kate.

Kate was looking at him sideways and stomping her feet on the stone to keep warm. She looked like she wanted to ask him something.

His phone buzzed again, then two more buzzes in quick succession. He shut off the ringer and checked the screen. Aunt Holly, his sister Dahlia, and Giovanna, his former boss in New York, (who also happened to be Dahlia's fiancé's mother) all had called within seconds of each other. Uncle may as well call. But he never called. Just got others to enforce the rules. He was feeling a little ganged up on.

"Kate, I need to go." Florian tugged down his hat, even though he didn't need to make sure his ears were covered. He shifted from foot to foot and eyed the Golden Gate Bridge in the distance. The fog now obscured its lights.

"Everything okay?" She eyed his phone.

He shoved the annoying thing into his pocket. "Yah, just a family drama."

"You need to deal with it? You okay?" She stepped closer to him.

"Yes. No. I just need to think." She smelled so good, but he didn't step toward her. He couldn't stop staring at that black smudge. What if the spark had landed on Kate and set fire to her clothing?

"About us?" she asked softly.

He glanced up at her and eyed her lips. "No. Kate, we're good. I just need to work out a few things. So I can stay."

"Oh." She stepped into his heat, flush against him. She kissed him on the lips, stepped back, and held out her hand. "So we're good." She stated. "And that means—"

"It means I'll be at the kitchen tomorrow to prep for the party." He smiled more brightly than he felt and took her hand. "We need to make a little girl's day tomorrow." Was he getting cold feet?

"And after that?" she whispered and squeezed his hand. "I guess I need to hear it. I feel—" She placed a hand on his heart and shrugged. "You feel distant to me."

He kissed her cheek. "Kate, we'll work it out." He just didn't know how. It was harder than he thought telling her outright who he was. The consequences—so much to lose.

He wanted to be with her, but...

"What if we don't?" she said, worry crinkling her forehead.

"We will. Let me sleep on stuff. We didn't get much sleep last night. I have to deal with—" He patted his pocket, shrugged, and gave her a quick peck on the lips. "Which way is the BART station?"

She pointed west downhill toward the bridge. "I can give you a ride."

"Sure, I'll walk you back to the party, then head home. Well, you'll walk me back. I have no idea how to get there." He blew out a breath.

"Why don't you come over?" She grinned and threw her arms around him.

"I don't think that's a good idea tonight." He touched her cheek. "And don't talk to Alex."

"Florian—" She swatted him on the shoulder. "I'll talk to who I want to."

"But don't let him take you home." He gave her sidelong glance, a mock frown on his face.

"Florian, I didn't know you were the jealous type."

"I didn't know I was either." He stared at her. "Would you consider me old fashioned if I told you that—" He eyed her lips. Her face glowed. Or maybe it was the magic shimmering around them. He wasn't conscious of sparking it, yet there it was.

She kissed him hard. "That what? You sure you don't want to come home with me?"

"That you're mine." He kissed her again, body against body. When he came up for air, she laughed and she was glowing.

"Oh, Florian, I feel like a half-baked cake." She rested her forehead on his. "Good but not complete. But I guess we can't solve all the world's problems in one night."

"Or on one stroll." He kissed her neck. "And we didn't even come up with a new cupcake recipe."

"Oh, I did. Two in fact. Donut cupcakes and chocolate cookie cupcakes."

He chuckled. "My favorite things. I can't wait to taste them." He turned in the direction in which they came and gestured. "That way?"

"I'll take us on another path back." She grinned.

"To confuse me, so I can never find this place again?"

She giggled. "You'll always be able to find the Campanile."

He smiled and waved his hand toward the clock tower. It chimed and lamplights blew out. But they were already walking away and out of range of any flying sparks. Luckily the place was deserted. His phone buzzed, but he ignored it and realized several things. He could control his magic. The harmless consequences seemed not so random. Twice he made the bells chime, and twice the lamplights blew. And he didn't care so much right now about revealing his magic. He wanted to show Kate what he could do. Maybe she'd just accept this part of him and he wouldn't have to state outright his true identity. Then he could have his cupcake and eat it too.

He could stay with Kate, have a life with her, and keep his magic. He shivered.

Kate threw an arm around him and pulled him close as they walked down the path into a dark wooded area.

A man could dream, couldn't he?

Chapter Thirteen

Kate didn't know what had just happened. What had Florian just shown her? That he was magic? That he did magic? How could any of that be?

Hands clasped, his grip was warm, his stride steady with hers, they walked side by side in silence, back to her brother's fraternity. Despite the strange things she'd witnessed back on campus, she felt at ease and calm with Florian, unlike anything she'd ever experienced with anyone before. And yet, his awe-inspiring and overwhelming show with the Campanile bells—was it real, or was this some elaborate trick? She didn't know what to think, and yet her heart urged her not to think. To just feel. And it felt right to be with him. As they strolled up Bancroft Avenue, the bay at their backs, she snuck a peek at him.

He seemed deep in his own thoughts, his cute red ski cap with a white pom-pom flopped over to one side.

She squeezed his hand. He squeezed back. She wanted things to work out. She really did. She blew out a breath. A rosy future bloomed in front of her, one with Florian in it. But she had to be realistic. What if he didn't stay? She blinked at the sudden surge of tears threatening to break and lifted her chin in the cold night air. She'd figure things out, adjust, take more risks. If there was anything that she'd learned in the short time Florian had been in her life was that she could stand to take more risks in her business, as she did with her heart, and trust more.

Fifteen minutes later, they stood in front of the fraternity. In the front yard, ground lights spotlighted the pretty sculptures ringing a low fountain. The low lights put in relief the fragrant sagebrush and lantana bushes.

"I'll walk you to your car," Florian said, breaking their silence.

"I need to go in and say good bye to my brother."

Silhouettes of college students filled the living room. Laughter spilled out as a couple slipped out the front door, hand in hand, smiled knowingly at each other, and strolled up the hill.

"You're a good sister." Florian let go of her hand.

She shrugged. "Sometimes." She gave him a half smile. "Come in with me and let's—" She shrugged again. "I don't know—cuddle on the couch."

"Are you trying to seduce me, Ms. Delore?"

"Yes." She leaned into him.

He leaned in and kissed her.

She sighed and leaned closer, yearning for more.

He was the first to end the kiss. He caressed her cheek. "I'll come in and say good bye too. But no couch, *grá*, love."

Florian stepped into the fraternity house with Kate. The living room was still full of college students, laughing, drinking soda, and—he chuckled—playing cards. He saw at least three games going on around the room.

Hank wasn't in the living room. Kate grabbed his hand. "Come on." He followed her to the billiard room. More people playing pool and others watching the games on several tables. Alex, Kate's ex was playing with a young man sporting a backwards baseball cap. Alex waved at them.

Kate waved. Florian stiffened and frowned.

Kate let go of his hand. "I just want to say bye to him."

"I'll come with," Florian said.

"You don't need to."

"I do."

Kate gazed at him, a look of confusion on her face.

"I told you, Kate, you're mine. I just discovered I'm the jealous type. I'm staying with you."

"I—" She snapped her mouth shut, though the rouge of some strong emotion colored her cheeks. She glanced at Alex. "Hey Alex, see you later. Nice to see you. Enjoy your stay here."

Alex looked up from the shot he was preparing. He looked between Florian and Kate, said something to his playing companion, then sauntered over. He reached out a hand to Florian. "Good night. It was a pleasure meeting the man who stole Kate's heart." Alex's strong grip and how he was holding on for a little too long, as if he were challenging him, compounded with the fact that he stared down at Florian from a height advantage of fifteen and a quarter centimeters or six inches.

"I didn't steal anything." Steam boiled in Florian's chest. He felt the surge of magic leap before he was aware of it. Someone yelped. A billiard ball crashed to the floor. Florian broke his gaze from the stare down with Alex, yanked his hand out of the man's grip, and scanned into the billiards room.

The baseball hat guy was shaking his hand, staring at the ball on the floor, and swearing. "The ball smashed into me."

"I didn't see anything," said a student watching.

"What did you do?" Kate whispered to Florian. She turned to Alex and said, "Bye. I need to find my brother." She tugged Florian. "Come on. What did you do?"

Florian shook his head. "I don't know." Under his breath he said, "That's never happened before. Oh bells." Not good. Not good at all. His phone buzzed. He shut it off. Turned the whole thing off. He didn't want to hear it. Didn't want to hear the warnings, the worry, and scolding. He was done.

He hadn't been trying to use magic. He didn't mean to hurt anyone. He was just so pissed at Alex. His body vibrated. Was this what his aunt had been warning him about—the part about harm to others? And the spark that almost set Kate alight back by the clock tower.

He followed Kate toward the kitchen. Hank wasn't there either. She pulled out her phone and called him. "Hey Hank, where are you? We want to say goodbye." She was quiet for a moment, and then said, "Okay. We'll be right up."

She switched off her phone. "He's upstairs in the library."

"During a party?"

"Yah, he's weird that way, says he's looking something up."

He tromped up the stairs with Kate. They entered the honest to goodness library, four walls covered in floor-to-ceiling shelves filled with books. He smiled, unbuttoned his coat, warm from the hike up the stairs, yanked off his hat, and stuffed it into his pocket.

Hank glanced up from the book he was reading, *The Fall of the Roman Empire.* He smiled at Kate and his eyes widened when he looked at Florian.

Florian faltered in his stride and mussed his crazy hair as a cover to check his ears. Bells. They were still pointy, not yet warmed up to revert to Human shape. And Hank saw.

Florian shook his head, hoping Hank would get the message to not say anything. The power was lost when an elf actually spoke his or her true identity, not if someone saw something. Like Hank had or Kate seeing his magic in action. Things were getting complicated though. The Delore siblings knew something, though they didn't really know what they saw.

Hank nodded, as if he understood not to say anything.

Florian slipped his hat back on for good measure. Hopefully, Hank wouldn't press him on it. Florian approached Hank. "Study hall versus party and study hall wins, eh?"

Hank grinned. "I just wanted to look something up. Julien challenged me. He's always doing that, acting like he was there or something. Nuts!" He glanced at his sister and grinned. "So you two left for a lover's stroll and didn't tell me."

"Because I tell you about all my lover's strolls." Kate swatted him in the shoulder.

Hank stood. "Love you, too, sis."

Kate leaned in and kissed him on the cheek. "Thanks for the party. It was—interesting. Interesting good." She glanced at

Florian, and then gave her brother a quick hug. "But why did you invite Alex?"

Florian frowned and stuffed his hands in his coat pocket. Just the mention of that man's name set his blood to boil. He scanned the bookshelves to distract himself, but listened to every word of Kate and Hank's conversation.

"Why not? You guys dated for four years. He's my friend too," Hank said.

Florian glanced up.

Hank continued. "I get it now. I didn't know about you two. I mean, I thought maybe, you know, but I didn't want to presume. I mean are you guys exclusive now? That was fast."

"Little brother, nosy much."

"Always in your business, big sister."

Florian stuck out his hand to Hank. "Thanks, man."

"Hey, sure." Hank shook his hand. "I didn't know you guys were serious. Sorry about that." He waved his hand in a dismissive gesture. "If I had known—"

"But you didn't." Florian shrugged, but tightened his hands into fists hidden in his pockets.

"He's a piece of work," Hank said.

"Who does he think he is, with that curl on his forehead? Superman?" Florian said through a clenched jaw.

"I know, right?" Hank slapped Florian on his shoulder. "Just forget about it. He's not worth it." Hank pulled him in for a half-hug. "She's with you. Do right by her. Or she'll slug you."

Florian chuckled and shook his head. "I haven't seen that side of her."

Once they were downstairs and heading out the front door, Kate asked him in a low voice. "What was all that about?"

"Guy talk."

"Pantomime and grunts are a language I'll never understand."

"We men have to have some things to ourselves."

"I guess." Kate reached for his hand as they stepped out the door. "You still don't want to come home with me. We'll both be at the kitchen tomorrow..." She swung their joined hands between them.

"Just a ride to BART, milady, will suffice."

She sighed, released his hand, and wandered over to the short statues and fountain. She said something he couldn't understand.

"What?"

She turned to him. "It's Latin for 'Loyal, Steadfast and True'." She smiled a little wistfully.

They walked in silence to her car, parked a block away. Was he true to her if he didn't actually tell her his true identity?

Chapter Fourteen

Saturday, December 6

The next morning at the late hour of 9 a.m., Florian was waiting at the kitchen door when she arrived. He greeted her with a chaste peck on her cheek, and her stomach dropped. Maybe things had changed between them. She unlocked the door and they stepped in. He tied on his apron, accepted the coffee she made for him, and was setting out supplies for the party cupcakes they were to make. She waited until she'd had her morning cup of coffee and then turned to him. She cleared her throat nervously. "So how did it go? With your family? Is everything okay?" She cleared her throat again. "Did you—Did you get things straightened out?"

Florian pursed his lips, and then licked them. "Can we just focus on the baking?" He leaned over and kissed her on the cheek again.

Kate opened her mouth and snapped it shut again. He said things would work out. She just needed to bide her time. She blew out a breath. Besides, he was right. They had a lot to prepare for the party. If she impressed this mother, she was sure there'd be a lot more kids parties in her future. "Then we talk in—" She glanced at her phone to gauge the time and calculate all the baking. "—In two and a half hours."

"Give or take," Florian said and plopped the measuring cups on the counter. He glanced at her, a softness in his gaze, and handed her a large mixing bowl. "I'll do wet and you do dry, then we mix?"

Her cheeks flushed. "We're good."

Florian laughed. "We're good."

Two and a half hours later plus thirteen minutes, Kate sighed with satisfaction and leaned against the counter. They didn't need to be at the party until 2 pm. The kitchen was once again clean, the cupcakes ready, and in the fridge. The van was even packed. They'd done it. The two of them. Together.

Florian pulled something wrapped from his backpack. He had a half smile on his face. "I have something for you."

She hadn't even noticed he had a bag with him this morning—he usually carried nothing after the first day—so focused she'd been on other things, like matters of the heart.

He handed her the wrapped item, trying to hide his grin.

She reached for it, then paused, eyeing what looked like a sandwich wrapped in wax paper. "What is it?"

"What? You don't trust me," he said in a mock outraged voice, a hand over his heart.

"Of course I do," she said.

He turned his expression neutral, grin gone. "But you want to know what's inside first before you accept it."

She shrugged. "I like to know what I'm jumping into before I—" She narrowed her eyes at him. "Who am I unwrapping, you or the sandwich?"

"Both," he said with a straight face. He still had the sandwich held out to her.

"A test. I see. To see how much of a risk taker I actually am." She nodded and shifted from foot to foot. If she wanted a relationship with him, she needed to accept him, all of him, without necessary knowing everything about him.

He set the wrapped sandwich on the counter between them and said nothing.

"Can I smell it?" She smiled, hoping he would too, and they could move back to just talking about sandwiches.

"I thought you wanted to talk?" Florian said, his gaze still neutral.

"Yes, I do, but when you offered food—I thought we'd go out for lunch. My treat. Then talk." She was avoiding. She did that when she was nervous. What reason did she have to be nervous? Oh yah, this thing between them, it was a big deal.

Florian crossed his arms in front of his body and leaned a hip against the counter. "Okay. But I thought it was talk first, eat second."

"I changed my mind. I'm hungry." She eyed the over four-inches thick rectangular sandwich.

"Me too." He considered her, frowning. "Taste it and tell me what you think."

"I've already tasted the wares." She stepped toward him and placed a hand on the sandwich.

He chuckled and watched her, amusement in his gaze.

She waited. When he said nothing else, she pulled the sandwich toward her. He placed his hand on hers, stopping her from snagging it. "What?"

"What if you don't like it?" He eyed their hands.

"I love everything you cook," she said. "You always know how to balance all the ingredients, so nothing overpowers anything else."

He didn't budge, his warm palm atop the back of her hand. He said nothing.

Ah. He meant himself.

Guess they were having it now.

Kate turned her hand to grip his and stepped toward him. Though they were the same age, both twenty-five years old, she suddenly felt so much older than he was. Perhaps she'd had more experience in relationships than he'd had. She'd been with Alex for four years. Florian hadn't mentioned any previous relationships. She hadn't asked. He couldn't be that inexperienced. He was quite good in bed and a great kisser.

He was searching her face, uncertainty writ on his wrinkled brow and in his eyes.

"What are you asking me?" she said softly. She didn't want to startle him or say the wrong thing.

He glanced at the sandwich and back at her with a wry smile. "Since when is my love life like a sandwich?"

"I'm sure it's a very delicious sandwich." She held out her other hand and stepped closer to him.

He grabbed her outstretched hand, inched closer to her, and brushed her cheek. "You have something there. Flour or sugar." He licked his palm. "Sweet. Like you." He pulled her the last inch to him.

Body against body, she gazed up at him. His lips were parted, delicious. She kissed him, the warmth of his body heating her from the inside out. He met her passion with his own.

When they broke apart, she sighed. "I love everything about you," she breathed. "Yes, to your sandwich and all of you."

Florian's eyes went wide and he leaned in for another kiss. He blinked. Was that tears she saw? He pulled her closer for a hug and then rubbed her back. "I'll just do this then and all will be well."

"Mmmm. All is well. There." She shifted so he could rub the knot that was lodged between her shoulder blades, much smaller though than before he'd presented himself at her cart. Was that on Monday, only five days ago?

She waited for him to say more and listened to the comfortable silence, melting under his expert touch. She felt surrounded by a warm tingly current. She opened her eyes, not realizing she'd closed them and gasped.

There was something enveloping them, golden, shimmering, vibrating. "What is it?" she breathed.

Florian stilled his massage and opened his eyes. They widened in surprise. Then he smiled at her. "Beautiful, isn't it?"

His phone buzzed on the counter.

She jumped.

He ignored it.

"Florian?" She searched his face.

He gazed openly back at her, but didn't reply.

Should she push him for a straight answer?

"Is it magic? But that can't be. Or can it?" She blew out a breath and shook her head. "I don't know what to think. But ... I know the impossible can become possible."

"Yes, that about sums it up." Florian nodded and smiled broadly at her.

She waited but he didn't say more.

"You said you had some family things to work out, to deal with," she prompted.

He rubbed her back absently. "I want to stay here with you, but I am also really attached to my other commitment." He pulled her close and hugged her, then leaned back. "I want both. I want the impossible. I can't have both. I want you—to stay here and play—" He grinned. "I mean, help you in building your business—with you—one hundred percent."

"It would be so much fun!" She exclaimed. She wanted that. She didn't realize how much she wanted a partner in her business and in her life until she met Florian.

"Fun is good." He smoothed his hands down her back and tickled her sides.

"Hey!" She jumped and giggled. "Stop!"

He grinned and stilled his dancing fingers.

She hugged him. "I didn't realize—" She blew out a breath.

"What?"

She pulled back to gaze up at him. "Well, just how much I wasn't having fun. Until you showed up at my cart five days ago."

"Five days." He gazed at her lips. "And that's it. I need more time."

"For what?"

"To make things work, silly." He beeped her on the nose.

"Hey!" She swatted his hand away. "Things are working." She peered around the clean kitchen. "What is there to work out? Let's just get on with our lives making beautiful cupcakes together."

"Is that a proposal?" His expression sobered.

She felt her cheeks flush. "Maybe. Yes." Her heart accelerated as if she'd just gulped down one of her Mexican chocolate spicy cupcakes too fast. "What if it is?"

"We need an exit clause then," Florian said.

"What?" She stepped out of his warm embrace. The gold shimmer was gone. She wasn't sure when it had disappeared. "You're talking about an exit when we've barely begun." She stomped away toward the door, spun to face him, and crossed her arms on her chest. Her cheeks flushed with heat. Her body vibrated so hard she was shaking. She gulped, trying to find calming breaths.

"Sorry. It's just—" He waved his hand in the air, as if to brush away his words, and then scrubbed his clean-shaven face. He'd shaved. "My practical side coming through." He glanced around the kitchen as if looking for something, or for something to do. But they'd already cleaned the small space and the kitchen was spotless. Then he peered at her. "Kate, are you okay?"

Something softened in her. She blew out a breath, feeling the heat release out of her as if she were a balloon. "I was wondering where your practical side was," she said with a shaky voice.

He cracked a smile. "You just made a joke, right?"

"I like your practical side," she said and fanned her face.

"That is fortunate because my practical side needs more time to make both things work." He picked up a cloth and refolded it, then dipped it in water. "I want to hear your plans for expansion. I want to succeed at the magic show this afternoon." He held out the cloth to her, a concerned look in his gaze. "What if I flop and my party magic show career is over before it's begun?"

"You won't flop." She strode back to him and took the cloth, patting her face. "What do you need to help you make both things work?"

He took the cloth from her, rinsed it in water, squeezed out the excess, and refolded the cloth on the counter, all without meeting her gaze. "I'm not sure. I need to have things figured out by December twenty-first."

"Why that date?" She stepped closer to him.

He blew out a breath. "That's when I'm supposed to be on a plane to return home."

"Right. You told me before—us." She leaned up against the counter in front of him and beside the unopened sandwich. "I don't want you to go."

He cupped her cheek. "I know. I don't want to. I just need to—" He shrugged. "Make the impossible work."

She slid into his welcome arms. "I really wanted to storm out of here. I got all hot. That was weird."

"Which part?"

"The heat and intense urge to leave. I get frustrated, but usually not like that."

He squeezed her into a fierce hug. "But you're fine now, right?"

"Yes," she squeaked out.

He hugged her tighter. "I don't want anything to happen to you."

"Why would anything happen to me?" She wriggled out of his tight embrace and examined his face.

He shook his head and shrugged. "I don't know." He brushed his red curls out of his eyes and blinked. "I just don't want anything to happen to you. You're too important to me."

"That feeling that when you love someone the thought of losing them is too painful?" she said softly and cupped his cheek.

"Yes."

His lips were right there, so she had to kiss them.

Her phone beeped. He broke off the kiss. "What's that?"

"Lunchtime." She reached for his sandwich. "Let's eat."

As she stood in her tiny kitchen, holding his homemade sandwich, she realized she loved this, loved him. And wanted to spend many more days like this with him.

She gave him a quick kiss on the lips. "Thank you."

He gazed at her hungrily. "You're welcome."

Chapter Fifteen

A few hours later, Mrs. Winthrop greeted them at the front door of her Berkeley Hills home off of Grizzly Peak Boulevard. She waved them in and toward a large dining room with a big open space, and the table moved to one wall. Kate and Florian set up the savory cupcakes on plates. Kate set up her special cupcake stand for the sweet cupcakes. Once all the cupcakes were placed on it, it looked like a cupcake tree.

Kate heard the patter of little feet. Mrs. Winthrop said, "Ms. Delore, I'd like you to meet my daughter, Amber. She wanted to see her cupcake tree."

Kate turned and smiled at the girl. "Nice to meet you, Amber."

"It's pretty," Amber said.

"Thank you. I made it just for you."

The little girl nodded. "Because I'm nine now."

"Yep." Kate grinned at her and then at her mother. "The food is all set up here and the coffee and tea over there." She waved to the other small table she'd brought with them.

"Very nice." The mother nodded approvingly.

Now all she needed was for Florian's magic show to go well. She had not only Mrs. Winthrop to impress, but all the parents who brought their children to the party.

As if Mrs. Winthrop read her thoughts, she asked, "Where is your magician? Is he here?" She glanced around.

"Yes, he's here. Florian went out to the van to return the trays and change clothes."

Mrs. Winthrop made a noncommittal noise. "I'd like to meet him before he does the show and have him meet my daughter."

"Of course." Kate eyed her smart phone for the time. "As soon as he's back."

"Good. Guests should be arriving in fifteen minutes. I want to meet him before then." She scurried away before Kate could reply.

Ten nervous minutes later, Florian found her futzing with the cupcakes display. She jumped when he touched her shoulder.

"I didn't mean to startle you," he said.

She spun.

He was in a full tuxedo with a burgundy red cummerbund and matching bow tie and breast pocket handkerchief. A top hat finished off the classic magician look.

She caught her breath. "You look—great. We match. I had no idea... Florian, so fun." She was in red burgundy jeans and a nice top, but all covered by her cupcake apron.

He bowed and spread out the cape with a burgundy under silk.

"Elegant."

He grinned and ruined the serious magician look.

"Mrs. Winthrop wants to meet you," she said. "And her daughter, Amber."

"I just met the husband. He let me in." He frowned. "I thought I saw Alex too." He shook his head and stuffed his hands into his pockets. "Maybe I'm seeing things."

"What's the husband's first name?" Kate looked off into the middle distance.

"David." Florian fiddled with his tie, shook out his cape, and paced the empty room.

She shrugged. "I don't remember David Winthrop being friends with Alex. But I didn't know all his friends..." She eyed him. "You'll do fine."

He stopped his pacing. "David did say he'd heard good things about you. Maybe from Alex."

"Maybe," Kate said absentmindedly and glanced around the empty dining room. Everything looked in order. "Let's go find Mrs. Winthrop."

Mrs. Winthrop was in the kitchen wiping down an already spotless counter. She eyed them seriously and nodded after a moment. "Stay here. I'll get my daughter."

Kate smiled and fiddled with her apron ties. Florian seemed to have recovered his bought of nerves and nodded regally.

"Relax, it'll be fine," he said.

Kate turned to him and straightened his bowtie even though it didn't need it. "Where did you get this?" she asked.

"I borrowed it from my uncle John. My aunt Holly altered it. I'm a little skinnier than my uncle." Florian chuckled.

"Now I'm the one who's nervous. This party is a big deal," Kate straightened his jacket. "Good word of mouth—"

Florian grabbed her hands. "It'll be fine. The food is great. The show will go well."

"But if this party doesn't go well—"

"It will." He kissed her lightly.

"But what if it doesn't." She eyed him, then reached for his handkerchief to square it, even though it was fine.

He chuckled. "Kate, whatever happens, we'll face it together. Together. You and me," Florian said and then kissed her lips, a chaste, quick peck. He stepped back and grinned. "Take a deep breath, relax, and put one foot in front of the other."

Just then, Mrs. Winthrop arrived with her daughter in tow.

Mrs. Winthrop addressed Kate. "Would you introduce us?" and gestured to Florian. An approving look was in her gaze. Finally.

"Please meet Florian the Great." That was the name they'd decided upon. "Florian, please meet Mrs. Winthrop and her daughter, Amber."

Florian nodded, swept his cape, and bowed at the waist. "I am quite pleased to meet you both."

The daughter asked, "Do you have a rabbit in your hat?"

"No," Florian said. "I don't do magic with animals."

"Why not?" she asked.

"They don't like it," Florian replied.

She considered that, and then said, "Okay. We're going to play games, then have the savory cupcake bites. Then your show, and then eat the cupcake sweet tree. I made a schedule." She held up a piece of paper written in child block letters.

"Very organized," Florian said.

"So please enjoy the party until your show," Amber said, still holding up the schedule. "This one is for you."

Florian took her schedule and nodded. "Thank you, and I will, Amber. Happy birthday."

"It's not my official birthday until 2:22pm," she said. "That's during the magic show."

"I'll be sure to wish you happy birthday then."

She nodded and then asked, "Can you do real magic?"

Florian gazed at her and said nothing for a moment, and then said, "I can."

She nodded again. "Good. I was just checking, because not every magician is doing real magic. Sometimes their tricks are magic, but sometimes they're just tricks."

Kate felt Florian stiffen at her side. He said nothing.

"Sometimes," Kate said, and hoped that would appease her.

The front doorbell rang. The little girl nodded sagely and walked away with her mother to greet guests.

"I hope your tricks will satisfy her. I had no idea how sophisticated she was," Kate said.

Florian placed a hand on her shoulder. "It'll be fine. How many tricks can she know? Plus, I'll make it fun and entertaining. That's the point, right?"

Kate nodded and smoothed down her apron.

Girls and boys peeked their heads into the dining room on their way to the playroom. Parents smiled at her. One asked if he could have a coffee. Kate nodded and waved toward the self-serve coffee and tea table.

Other parents wandered in and out, admiring the cupcake table and helping themselves to beverages.

She blew out a breath and replenished supplies as needed. This party was going to work. And be fun, she reminded herself.

At 2 p.m., Florian took the stage, really the front of the dining room that faced west. He'd pulled shut the curtains, so the afternoon sun wouldn't backlight him and make him hard to see. Twelve children, including the birthday girl, sat in folding chairs, gazing up at him expectantly. Parents stood behind with coffee, tea, and savory cupcakes in hand. Kate stood there too, in her cute apron with Kate's Cupcake Cart and her logo splashed across the fabric. His heart felt huge and full of bubbly.

He smiled at the children and started his show with a big scarf trick, pulling his handkerchief out of his breast pocket and having each child grab hold of it and pass it to his or her neighbor.

The white handkerchief became a rainbow-colored scarf, growing longer and longer. The children giggled as the scarf kept going, getting longer as it snaked around the children and across the chairs. He had the birthday girl take the end and give it back to him. The other end was still in his pocket.

"Okay, everyone, snap your fingers, like this." He had them snap and snap, so he had a room full of snapping children. Even some of the adults joined in. "Wonderful," he said, and stopped snapping and spread his arms wide. The rainbow scarf had disappeared and his white handkerchief was back in its place.

"Ooh, ahh!" The children said.

"What happened?" One boy asked, younger than the rest.

"How did you do that?" one girl asked.

"Yay!" the birthday girl said and clapped. "More!"

The other children clapped and so did the parents.

He waved his hand and bowed. Then he dramatically showed them his empty sleeves of his tuxedo coat, and then with a flick of his wrist, revealed a wand.

He pretended he was conducting. "Can't you hear it?" He hummed the 1812 Overture.

Some of the parents and children hummed along.

He finished with a crescendo and fanned out a deck of cards with his other hand.

The birthday girl smiled. "Ooh, card tricks! I like those. Those are good ones."

Florian smiled at her and had her pick a card. He took her and her friends through a few tricks, using sleight of hand, and having cards appear under the children's' seats and behind their heads. Amber laughed and clapped her hands. Things were going well. The children were laughing and giggling at his silly jokes. The parents were smiling and clapping.

Kate stood by the cupcake table, smiling at him. Beside her was a familiar face. Wait. What? What was Alex doing here? He hadn't been imagining things.

Florian faltered in his movements, as he was pulling out a handful of balloons to blow up and make disappear.

Alex whispered something in Kate's ear. She smiled and nodded, gazing up at him, for just a moment too long in his opinion. He shoved his anger away, then puckered his mouth to blow up the balloons and blew. But on the rubber, not the balloon hole. Of course nothing happened. He opened his eyes wide and pantomimed confusion for the kids. They laughed.

He had to ignore Alex. He could do this.

He blew on the balloon again. Nothing happened again, so he turned around, with his back to the audience, and glanced over his shoulder and winked. Children giggled. He blew and blew dramatically raising and lowering his shoulders while he worked the balloon out of their view. He gazed over his shoulder again and glanced at Kate. She stood too close to Alex. He had an arm draped across her shoulders and was gazing at her like she was his dessert.

He clenched his hands, balloon in hand, and ignored the boiling in his chest. No, no. Thank goodness the balloon didn't pop. He spun to show off his handiwork and worked hard to paste a smile on his lips. He blew air out, pretending to be exhausted. The children laughed at his antics.

Just then, he heard a pop. It sounded like metal snapping. And then disaster splatted in front of him. In front of all of them.

The pretty sweet cupcakes flew in an arc. He could see what was going to happen. "No!" he said and held out his hand as if he was stopping traffic. He didn't know how he did it, but everything froze for a split second. But he couldn't maintain the freeze or reverse the arc of cupcakes.

So the worse that could happen happened. Cupcakes hit Mrs. Winthrop square in the face and chest. She'd been standing at just the wrong place to receive the brunt of the cupcake attack.

The room seemed to suck in a collective gasp of air. A keen whistle blasted as if air was being let out of a balloon. Only it wasn't a balloon. It was Amber. It was her high-pitched squeak that crescendoed into a squeal and then a scream.

"My cupcakes!" The birthday girl. He'd just ruined her birthday party.

Then the children began to cry and the adults shouting at him. Amber stared at him through her tears.

Only Mrs. Winthrop was silent, glaring at him, ignoring her husband and Alex, who were both handing her towels and napkins.

Then she turned to Kate and said through gritted teeth, "Get out."

Kate, her face white, said, "My-my stuff—"

"Now!" Mrs. Winthrop pointed toward the front door.

Kate nodded and glanced around. "I should help you clean up."

Mrs. Winthrop shook her head and pointed to the door again. Alex, not a smudge of cupcake on him, shrugged at her. "I'll take care of it."

"No," Florian said from where he stood and clenched his hands into a fist. But no one heard him. The two balloons he'd twisted into animals popped.

The birthday girl wailed harder. Florian opened his mouth to apologize, but Kate shook her head at him and gestured for him to follow her. What had he done?

In the ten seconds it took for him to rush out to the van, remorse flooded him. Kate yanked the door open and slid behind the driver seat of the van. She was panting and her face was red. He reached for the door. She locked the door and shook her head at him, her hands gripping the steering wheel. The windows were rolled halfway down.

"Was that you?"

"Kate, let me in," he said.

She glared at him. "Was that you?" she asked again.

"Yes. I'm sorry, Kate. I really am. Now unlock the door."

Flushed, she stared at him. He held her gaze.

She relented and unlocked the door. He hoped into his seat. "Thank you." And then, "Are you okay?"

She said nothing, rolled down her window to let in the cold afternoon air, and gunned the engine. The van rocked side to side as she rushed down small narrow streets toward the flat lands.

He struggled to latch his seatbelt, but managed before they'd gone too far.

Kate said nothing, didn't even look at him.

How was he going to fix this? Could he even?

After ten minutes, Kate stopped the van.

"Where are we?" Florian didn't recognize the streets.

"Get out." She looked straight ahead and not at him when she spoke.

"Kate—"

"Berkeley BART," she said.

The Berkeley train station.

He waited for her to say more or look at him. But she didn't.

He opened the door and stepped down from the van. "Kate, I am sorry."

She stared through the windshield. "I know, but get out."

"I'll call you."

"Don't."

"But what about working things out together?"

"I—Just go," Kate glanced at him, then straight ahead. "I need—need some space." Her face was still red.

"Kate, I'm sorry. It was just that Alex—"

She slapped the wheel. "No, Florian. You—" Now she looked at him, tears streaming down her face. She opened her mouth, then closed it, and shook her head. She waved her hand. "I have to go."

She revved the engine. Florian shut the door and watched Kate drive down the busy street into the grey, cold afternoon. At least he had his hat to cover his ears. Maybe he was better off without his magic.

Jealousy was such an intense emotion. And his magic had to be affecting Kate too. He had no idea how destructive he could be. The exploding cupcake disaster had never happened before.

He'd never been in love before. His aunt and all the others were right. The intended consequences were dangerous.

By all that was sacred and sparkly, he was in love with Kate Delore. And would probably never see her again. He'd made a real mess of things.

Chapter Sixteen

She'd made a real mess of things. Kate pulled her van into the parking lot before she remembered that she had nothing to unload except for a bunch of empty trays. She dried her cheeks and got to work with a heavy heart.

How was she going to fix things? Was it even possible? Why should she let one disastrous party ruin her relationship with Florian? She'd been just so upset, so she sent him away.

Twenty minutes later, she was walking home in the chilly afternoon. It was weird that she was done so early. It was weird not knowing what was next, as if the rug had been pulled out from under her. Weird maybe wasn't the right word for it. Heartbreaking was more like it... No, yes, her internal self felt all muddled. What she needed was a bath, some red wine, and maybe for dessert New York Super Fudge Crunch ice cream. Then she'd call Florian and they'd sort this out. There had to be a solution. Together they'd sort it out.

Hours later, Kate felt stir crazy. She'd called Florian and left him a voicemail apologizing for overreacting and could he please call her as soon as he got her message. That was two hours ago.

Normally, she'd be planning for Sunday, all the chores she liked to do, and the planning of the menu and production schedule for the week, but she felt up in the air. It was hard to focus on work with the mess of the party and her burgeoning relationship staring her in the face.

Wrapped in her pajamas and bathrobe, curled on her couch, where only a few days earlier she'd flirted and kissed Florian, she fiddled with her smart phone. It was strange. The Winthrop family hadn't called, asking for their money back, even though her contract stated that she didn't do refunds only credit. Her insurance could handle whatever damages they might request. Supplies were expensive. None of the other families had called to cancel their parties, contrary to her expectations. Had Alex stepped in? Had he been the source of the referral in the first place?

She called Florian again, but he didn't pick up. She didn't know what to say, so she didn't leave a message. Who else could she call? All her girlfriends had stopped calling months ago when she stopped being able to hang out with them regularly and didn't have the time to initiate coffee or dinner dates. Mike was probably busy with his work at the shelter, and she'd lost touch with her professors and entrepreneur colleagues. She really needed to reach out more often. There was no one she felt comfortable calling, except for Florian, and her brother.

Hank picked up on the first ring. "What's up, sis?"

"I've made a real mess of things, Hank." Kate was silent for a moment. A lump of tears grew in her throat. "And I don't know how to fix it."

"Boy trouble?" Hank said. "Want me to come over so you can cry on my shoulder and your little brother can step in and save the day?"

She smiled and wiped her cheek. "Over the phone is fine."

"What happened? Did you and Florian have a fight?"

Kate sighed and told him what happened at the magic show and cupcake party.

"Wait. What? Are you telling me Florian used magic to make the cupcakes go flying? No way. Are you sure?"

"I don't know. I think so. I don't know how he did it, but he admitted that he did."

"Why? He couldn't have purposefully sabotaged the party. He doesn't seem like that kind of guy."

"He isn't." Kate took a sip of water. She'd decided to pass on the wine. She needed a clear head.

"Then why."

"I think it was because of Alex," Kate said, staring into her glass, without seeing it.

"What was Alex doing there?" Hank asked, exasperation in his voice. "Is he stalking you?"

"No. Why do you say that?"

"Well, why was he there?"

"I asked him the same thing. Turns out he's good friends with the father of the family. He probably recommended me to them."

Her phone beeped. It was text. Her heart thudded. Maybe it was from Florian.

"Hold on, Hank."

She checked her phone's text messages. It was from Alex. Her heart sank.

I helped clean up. Are you okay?

She closed the text program without answering.

"Who is it? Florian?" Hank asked

"No. It's from Alex. Do you think he wants me back?"

Hank said nothing.

"Hank, you there?"

"It's just that, before the party, Alex asked after you. Asked if you were dating anyone."

"Well, I hope you told him that I was."

"This was before the party. I told him that you weren't."

She swore. "What? Why didn't you tell me this yesterday? It's none of his business. He could have just asked me directly. The nerve—"

"Whoa nelly. Hold your horses."

"Why? He pisses me off."

"Uh, sis. I think you were giving him mixed signals."

"Oh." Maybe she had. "I was just happy to see him...It'd been a while." She tapped her glass. "Old habits. What a mess. I just—"

Hank interrupted, "I don't want the juicy details. I'm not one of your girlfriends."

"I know, Hank. I called you for advice. Isn't that what brothers are good for?" She glanced around her small apartment, noticing how empty it looked.

"We're good for something." Hank blew out a breath. "I'm no expert in love or business, but if you want my know-it-all opinion, I say call Florian and work it out with him."

"I did. Twice. He didn't answer."

"Oh."

"Oh, what? You're no help."

"You'll work it out. You're smart. What do you want me to say?"

She blew out a breath. "That's good. Keep it coming."

"Um, be patient and don't give up on love."

"Those are both good. You should open up an advice column, little brother."

"My frat brothers do turn to me for advice from time to time because I sound like I know what I'm talking about, even though I don't."

She sighed. "I think it's time for me to get some ice cream."

"And risk your heart. I just had to throw that in there," Hank said.

She nodded and sipped her water.

Hank said, "Sis?"

"I'm here. I thought I was good at taking risks. I thought I was doing that."

"Well, maybe with your heart. But what about with your business? You'd probably grow it faster if you took more risks and let go of some control.

"Listen to you giving me business advice," Kate joked.

"No, I'm just an analyst."

"Right." She snorted.

"I am. Haven't you read my blog?"

"An advice blog? No, I've too busy running a business."

"No, on lots of things. Life, relationships, history. Better get busy, sis."

She chuckled again.

"Better," Hank said.

"What?"

"Laughter. You're laughing. That's a good sign. You've really lightened up lately. Florian's a good influence on you."

"Except for today."

"Yah. Except for today." Hank fell silent.

"What am I going to do?"

Hank blew out a breath. "Call him again. Don't give up. Persistence. Okay? You taught me that." He sounded exasperated with her, but he was probably just messing with her.

"Okay. Geez."

"You asked, I answered. There was no guarantee you'd like my advice. You just wanted to hear what you already knew."

"Who are you and what did you do with my nerdy immature baby brother?"

"I grew up, sis. Get used to it. I'll be going to grad school next year and then you really won't be able to call me your immature baby brother. But I'll always be nerdy. Count on that."

She smiled. "Nice speech, Hank."

"You like it? I've been practicing it since I was ten," Hank paused and then said. "You got this, sis."

Kate shook her head. "No, I don't. But thanks. For the first time in my life, I can see that I don't have it all together." She stared at her empty glass. "Thanks, little brother. I'm going to hang up now and call Florian again."

"Good luck." Hank clicked off.

Kate set her phone down on the coffee table. She walked to the kitchen, refilled her glass from the water carafe beside the sink, and drank the whole glass standing there. She stared out her small kitchen window at the neighbor building across the alley. Lights flickered on as dusk fell. She needed to get out of her apartment to think. She changed into jeans and her favorite long-sleeved shirt. Bundled in her coat, she stepped out into the brisk night.

If Florian didn't contact her tonight, would he call tomorrow? That was Sunday. She needed to prep for the workweek, shop for supplies, and plan the menus. What if he didn't contact her until tomorrow night? Then it would be too late to make plans for the week. Because what if he called to— she didn't know—call her a ninny and say he was outta here.

She huffed as she walked uphill toward the golf course behind the neighborhood. Her breath puffed white in front of her. She clasped her phone in her pocket, turning it over and over in her palm. In just a short while, she'd come to rely on him. He was into her. She was into him. He wanted to stay. But—but—she'd really messed things up. She passed an empty golf course and trudged alongside the road.

Reality stared her in the face. She didn't want to be alone anymore. She didn't want to be alone in her business either. And she was willing to risk her heart and everything to be with Florian.

She pulled out her phone and clicked Florian's number. It rang. He still wasn't picking up. This time she left another message.

"Florian, please pick up. I am so sorry. I—was such—I was so stupid. I felt so angry, but that was no excuse. Please call me." I need you in my life, she thought, but couldn't say. She blew out a breath and continued. "I don't understand about this magic stuff. Seems risky. Hard to control. But we can handle it, together, right?" She stopped walking and turned to face west. The lights of Oakland sparkled below. "Please call me. Tonight."

She clicked off the phone and picked up the pace and walked back down the hill. Time to get her ice cream and dinner fixings and contemplate her next move. Like drive into the city and show up at Florian's door.

Fifteen minutes later she was standing in line with her ice cream and box of gluten-free Amy's Mac n' Cheese when her phone rang. She fumbled for it. It wasn't Florian calling, but a local number she didn't recognize. She paid for her groceries, nodded her thanks to the cashier, and answered. "Kate's Cupcakes, can I help you?"

"Hi, um, I'm Jane Lee."

The mother for next week's party. The cancellations were starting. Her stomach dropped. She shouldered her groceries and headed home. "Hi, Mrs. Lee."

"Call me, Jane."

"Oh, okay, Jane. How can I help you?"

"I'm sorry for calling so late, but I heard through the grapevine what happened at Leslie Winthrop's party, and well, I'm just calling to lend you my support. I'm sure it was an accident, and I just wanted to let you know that I still want you to do my daughter's party next week."

Kate blinked and faltered in her step. It wasn't that late, was her first thought. Her second was, thank you.

"Ms. Delore, are you there?"

"Call me Kate. What exactly did you hear?" Kate resumed walking, her heart beating too fast. She couldn't believe her stroke of luck.

"That there was an equipment malfunction and the pretty cupcakes splatted all over Leslie," Jane said, her voice full of glee. "Is that what really happened?"

Must be some kind of mom rivalry.

"I'm afraid so. I'm checking my cupcakes stands." Kate made a mental note to do so the next day.

"Well, I trust you. I know these things happen. I hope your insurance is good. But maybe just do trays for my party. It doesn't have to be fancy. Emily is just six, after all. She's not all caught up in appearances and prestige," Jane said.

"Thanks, Jane. I really appreciate it," Kate said, and then fell silent. She didn't know what else to say. She wasn't up to small talk at this hour. Body needed some time off.

"I'll let you go, Ms. Delore, Kate. See you next Saturday."

"Sure. And thank you for your vote of confidence, Jane."

"My pleasure." Then Jane clicked off. It sounded like she wanted to say more, like how happy she was to one-up Leslie Winthrop, but decided against it.

Thank goodness. Kate just wanted to make her customers happy, repair what she could, and move on. But move on exactly how? She didn't know, and for the first time in a long time, she was thinking that maybe that was okay.

Ten minutes later, she was back in her apartment and served herself desert first. She set the water to boil for her quick pasta. She put away the rest of her groceries and set her phone beside her pint of New York Super Fudge Crunch. She took a big bite and savored the sweet, nutty, creamy, cold make-all-things-better salve to her heart. Then she put her spoon down, hit Florian's number again, and put the phone on speaker.

His number rang a few times and then went to voice mail. His cheery voice greeted her and invited her to leave a message, inviting her to have a delicious and magical day. She smiled at his recorded greeting and felt her heart constrict at the same time.

"Hi Florian, another message from me. I didn't notice your voicemail message before. It's sweet." Like you, she wanted to say. She cleared her throat. "Call me. I'm sorry for-for... Please just call me," she said again and clicked off.

She put away the ice cream and turned off the water for the pasta. She didn't feel like eating. She needed to burn off some steam. Clear her head. Not think for a change. She changed into her running clothes and headed out for a run in the hills by the golf course.

He may never call her back. She hated that possibility, but there was nothing she could do about it right now. Maybe it was okay that for one night she didn't have her whole life figured out. Not even a little bit.

Chapter Seventeen

Saturday evening, hours and hours after Kate had dropped him off in Berkeley to take the train back to San Francisco, Florian hoisted Uncle John's bike over his shoulder and hiked up the three flights of stairs to the apartment. It was 8 p.m. He'd gone on a long ride. His aunt and uncle were out. He wasn't sure where. He checked his phone for messages. He'd left it home, needing to get away from it all.

There were four calls from Kate. Two were messages. He pressed "play message" and heard her sweet voice apologizing and asking him to call her about five times. He smiled. He hit "call back," kicked off his shoes, and headed toward his small bedroom.

"Hi!" she answered. She sounded breathless.

"You okay?" he asked.

"Yah. I was just running, jogging. Well, really running. Listen, Florian, I am—I feel bad—I'm sorry." She huffed out. Then she was quiet.

He jumped in to fill the silence. "Kate, no, it was my fault. How can I make it up to you? I can pay for the supplies that got ruined. Refund the customer. Anything, name it."

"No, that's my job." She fell silent again. "Besides, I have insurance."

He heard cars and a distant siren. "You outside?"

"I'm just arriving home from my run," Kate said, still sounding a little breathless. "I'm home now."

The background noise dropped away.

"I know I made a mess of things. Do you want me to come in Monday?" he said and crossed his fingers, hoping she'd say yes. He paced the length of his ten-foot by ten-foot square room.

"Yes, of course. I—I—Can you come by tomorrow? 1 p.m. Lunch and talk. Work things out."

"Why not now?" Florian smiled.

He heard clunking noises and something crash.

"Everything okay over there?" Florian asked.

"Yay, it's just me throwing my shoes into the closet."

"Poor closet," Florian said.

"Poor shoes," Kate chuckled.

Florian laughed. "Okay, I'll bring the lunch for tomorrow."

"You don't have to do that—" she protested.

"It's the least I can do," he said. "And Kate?"

"What?"

"I am so sorry about what happened at the party today," he said.

"Did you do it on purpose?" Kate asked soberly.

"Ruin the party? No!" he said.

"Where you trying to hit Alex?" she asked.

"I wasn't trying to hit anybody. I wasn't conscious of—" He shut his mouth.

She blew out a breath. "I can't pretend to understand what's going on. I mean, how you were able to do that?"

He said nothing.

"Florian?"

"Yes?"

"We'll talk tomorrow," Kate said.

She sounded sad—her good mood gone—but he didn't know what he could do. He wasn't even sure they were a couple or had a future together, even though she said to come in Monday, and reminded him what he'd told her—that they would work things out together. He had to find a way to make it work—make them work and keep his magic intact. Or maybe he needed to let the magic go. Look at all the problems it was causing.

"Kate, take care. I'll see you tomorrow." I wish I could hold you, he thought, but didn't say.

"Okay." But she didn't hang up.

He waited.

Finally, she said, "I miss you."

"I miss you too, Kate," he said putting as much love as he could into his words.

She clicked off.

He'd cook up the best lunch he could and put love—without magic—into it.

Kate stared at her phone. She wanted to text him back and say that everything was going to be okay again. They'd work it out, but there was something he wasn't saying, pulling between them like too dry taffy. Could their new relationship handle the strain?

She picked up her phone and set it down again on the kitchen counter. She'd tie herself in knots again if she continued along these lines, and she'd just taken her run. She didn't want to exercise the confusion out of herself again. Instead, she jumped in the shower, and then slipped into bed with a good romance novel. That would take her mind off her own troubles for a while.

December 7, Sunday

The next morning Florian was up early cooking up a storm. Later—he wasn't sure how much time had passed—Aunt Holly entered into the kitchen and poured herself a cup of coffee.

"What are you making here?" Aunt Holly asked. "Food for an army?"

He surveyed the kitchen. "No, lunch for Kate and I. And for you and Uncle John. And a few days worth of lunches for all of us."

"Are you planning a double date?" Aunt Holly smiled.

"No. I don't know how to make food for just two people." Florian put away the jars he was done with. When he turned back, Aunt Holly was still standing there, her arms crossed in front of her. He busied himself with wrapping up the sandwiches and packing the coleslaw into portable containers.

"You can't keep ignoring my warning calls, Florian," Aunt Holly said finally.

Florian packed the backpack and then peered at her. "It's not like I have control of my magic, most of the time."

"So you have some control, and that's supposed to make it okay?"

"No. I know the rules. I just can't seem to control my magic when strong emotions are involved." Florian stood in the middle of the kitchen with a loaf of bread in one hand and a half a tomato in the other. Pressure weighed on his chest like an unbalanced refrigerator.

"You're going home soon—" Aunt Holly started.

"But what if I don't? What if I stay here, like you did?" Florian blurted out. He put away the food in the fridge, and turned to busy himself with wiping down the counters and putting away the remainder of the fixings and leftovers. He glanced at Aunt Holly when she said nothing. Her expression was thoughtful. "You're happy with your decision, right?" he asked.

She brightened. "Very happy. I was just thinking about what you'd be giving up."

"Let me worry about that." Florian wiped his hands on the dishtowel. "I just needed to hear that from you. Again."

"Sounds like you've made up your mind."

"I have, but I just need to talk to Dahlia. Is she still around? I've been so busy I haven't called her." Florian hoisted the lunch backpack onto his shoulders.

"Yes, she's jetting around with Liam." Aunt Holly smiled. "Ah, young love."

"She seems to have the best of both worlds. She gets to be a Master Elf and keep her magic and jet around the world with her Human," Florian said wistfully. He leaned against the counter and crossed his arms. "How did she manage that, Aunt Holly?"

"Is that what you want? With your cupcake girl?"

"Kate." Florian shifted the pack on his shoulders. "I can't keep lying to her. Yet, if I tell her..." Not to mention that the magic was getting out of hand, but he didn't want to tell Aunt Holly that. He'd really never hear the end of it.

"If you tell her who you really are, then you'll lose your magic and Elf status," Aunt Holly said, eyeing him calmly.

"But what about Dahlia?"

Aunt Holly shook her head. "You'll have to take that up with Uncle."

"I can't call him." He blew out a breath. Then he straightened. "Maybe I should do what Dahlia did and entice Kate to the North Pole." He shook his head. "I don't think a life up there would suit her."

Aunt Holly poured herself a cup of coffee, her back to him, and said, "Dahlia's was a special case, Florian. I don't think things work that way."

"How does it work?" Florian shifted the backpack on his shoulders.

"Again you'll have to take it up with Uncle."

"Okay, when I see him, I'll take it up with him." Florian pulled on his cap. "I could still visit the Pole, couldn't I? If I gave up my Elf status?" Florian shifted from foot to foot again. He wanted to get going, but he needed to finish this conversation with his aunt.

"Sure."

"But you've not gone back."

She shrugged. "The time hasn't felt right." Sadness flickered across her face and then was replaced with calm. "This is our home. We're happy here."

"And you don't miss magic," Florian stated more than asked.

"There's magic all around, if you know how to spot it."

He nodded. "And love is a kind of magic."

She smiled. "It is. Now go meet with your cupcake girl." She squeezed his arm and gave him a peck on the cheek.

He nodded soberly. He had to make things right between them, somehow. Kate was waiting for him to straighten things out. He kissed his aunt on the cheek in return and waved good-bye. On his walk to catch the Muni bus to the train to Oakland, he called Dahlia.

His sister picked up right away. "Florian! You naughty boy you! All that magic! Bet Aunt Holly has been on your case. Must be bad for her to rope us all into calling you." But she laughed, no sting or recrimination in her voice. She understood the appeal of magic and love.

"Hey, sis. I'm sure you're busy gallivanting around the world, discovering awesome toy ideas, but I need to ask you something." Florian tugged his hat down over his ears against the San Francisco chill brisk wind.

She laughed and he heard kissing noises. "Liam says hi! We're in Sacramento meeting with some young inventors."

"That's quite the life."

"Do you want me to put in a good word with Uncle so you can do something similar?"

"So that's how it works. Do you mean we can just ask Uncle to be able to stay in the Human world and still practice magic and be with our Human?" Florian stopped at the bus stop and shook his head. "I don't know, sis. I should do it myself."

She laughed. "I don't think it's that simple."

"So you putting in a good word won't do anything?"

"I honestly don't know. I just said that because, well, it couldn't hurt." She said something he couldn't hear.

"What's that?" Florian asked. His bus arrived. He hopped on, scanned his pass, and settled into a seat.

"Liam was just saying something funny."

"Okay, love birds. Try to stay on topic," Florian said.

Dahlia laughed. "Just you wait, little brother."

"I don't have to," he said softly.

"Ah!" Dahlia laughed.

"You're having way too much fun at my expense, sis. And you're not helping with any useful advice."

"You're going to have to figure it out on your own, Florian. Love will find a way." Dahlia paused, and then continued softly. "What do you want?"

"I want to bake and be with Kate."

"She's a winner."

"How do you know?"

"I met her and if you want to be with her, then she wins."

Florian smiled and got off the bus. "Sis, I got to go. You helped, I think."

"What are sisters for?" Dahlia laughed and said good-bye.

Florian smiled and shook his head at his sister's bubbly happiness. She'd been with Liam for two years, and it seemed like her happiness only blossomed more and more each time he heard from her.

Thirty minutes later, at midday, he was knocking on Kate's door. Just like he had six days previous when he'd come over to practice for the magic show.

She opened the door. "Hi," she said, a small smile on her lips, and waved him in, backing up in the small hallway to make room for his tall frame and large backpack.

He walked into the small kitchen and set his backpack on the counter. "Some of this needs to be refrigerated. Do you mind?" He zipped open the bag and emptied it.

"No." Kate stood there, so pretty in her jeans and dark green sweater.

Florian busied himself with putting the salad and dessert into the fridge.

Kate watched him and said nothing.

He'd been thinking how to approach the topic and blurted out, "If you could live anywhere in the world, where would you be?"

She gazed around her apartment and spread her arms. "Here."

"This place or this city?"

"I really like it here." She cocked her head sideways. "What about you? You've traveled to lots more places than I have."

Florian set the sandwiches on the counter and stashed his bag by the front door.

Kate slid into the galley kitchen. "Well?" She lifted a mug out of the cupboard. "Want some tea or—?" She grabbed a wine glass. "Wine?"

"Do you have any root beer?" He slid into a stool on the other side of the kitchen counter and eyed her lips. He hadn't even kissed her hello. That just wasn't right. He leaned toward her. "Come here."

Kate eyed him, and then turned away, setting the glass and mug down, and opened the fridge. She bent over to peer inside, offering him a nice view of her shapely behind. The tease. She straightened and peered over her shoulder at him. "I don't have any root beer. Want to walk over to the grocery store to get some?"

"No, I want to stay here with you. I just got here."

"No, I mean together. Walk and talk."

"No, I want to stay here. With you." Florian slid off the stood and came around the counter to Kate, standing in the narrow kitchen, blocking her exit. "I came all this way. Around the world."

She stood a few inches from him, not moving, looking up at him, at his lips. "I want you here."

"I'm here." He waited, his desire and love for her exploding in his heart, bubbling over.

"I've been so—" She stepped to be practically flush against him.

"Bossy," he whispered. He angled his head to kiss her.

"Muddled." She met him half way.

They kissed, soft and warm.

He pulled away slowly. "Was that clear?"

"Very. It's about the only thing that is," Kate said and wrapped her arms around him. "I feel like I'm free falling and you're there to catch me. But if you aren't here..."

"I'm here." He bent in for another kiss. They stood in the kitchen like that in each other's arm, hugging, swaying. Kate let out a sigh and slipped out of his arms, grabbing his hand. He let her tug him into the living room area and onto the loveseat. She sat at one end and him at the other, their legs woven over each other's.

"Can we have a meeting?" she asked.

"You're the boss."

"That's just it. I don't want to be the only boss. I want a life with you, a partnership." Kate held out a hand.

He took it.

"But there's something between us—a tightness." She shrugged.

"You don't know—" He gulped. "You don't know everything about me."

"You don't know everything about me, either. We can discover it all together." She sounded so hopeful and trusting.

He loved that about her. That she was ready and willing to take the leap. He needed to take the leap too and go all in. The magic was too out of control. He was starting to cause harm—at Hank's party and then at the girl's birthday party. He knew that now. He had to give it up. He squeezed her hand. "I haven't told you much about where I come from. Who I am."

He waited for a reaction.

"Is this about the magic?"

"Yes."

"Are you from the future or another dimension?" She joked.

He looked at their entwined fingers. "The later."

"What? Really?"

"You don't seem surprised." Florian disentangled his hand and his legs and stood. Then he paced the small living room. He stuffed his hands into his pockets to keep them from fluttering and throwing wayward magic.

"Florian, the world is full of unexplainable things." She held out her hand to him. "Come sit down with me." She patted the couch.

He faced her. "If I tell you all about me, I—" He shook his head. "It all changes for me. I can't have that other life." He puffed out a breath and focused on her. "I want to do that. Tell you about me, where I come from."

"Okay." She dropped her arm and nodded, frowning.

"I want to bake and that's what I get to do if I go home. Full time, in a prestigious and important position in my community. Highest honors." He shrugged. "Something I've been working toward for a long time."

"I know what that's like to work for something for so long." She squinted at him. "You said 'if.' "

"Yes. If I stay here with you, I give up that life. And the magic."

"You can't go back?"

"Maybe to visit. But I don't think I can reclaim my post later. Or my abilities. My window of opportunity closes on Christmas Eve." He sat back down on the loveseat and stared at the rug, not really seeing it.

Kate scooted closer to him and opened her arms to pull him into a hug. "I don't want you to give up your dream because of me and my dream," she whispered.

"It's my choice," he whispered back into her sweet-smelling hair and hugged her tight.

A loud thumping beat vibrated through him. His heart beat. He was surrounded by a faint whispering of a bubbling creek and the wind whistling through tree branches, as if they were in a forest meadow. So peaceful.

"What's that?" Kate said, leaning back, looking wide-eyed at him.

"My magic." He smiled, feeling sad and happy, all at once, his heart beating in time to the thumping he'd heard and felt. "I'm—"

"Making it happen," Kate said, interrupting him.

His phone buzzed in his back pocket. He'd learned and now kept the ringer off.

Another pretty ring sounded from somewhere else in the apartment.

Kate ignored it, so maybe it wasn't coming from this apartment.

He nodded. "Not exactly on purpose."

"It's wonderful."

"I'm—"

She held up her hand in the stop gesture. "Florian, don't tell me who you really are. I don't want you to lose your abilities, especially not your baking."

"I'll still be able to bake."

"But your magic—"

"Would be gone."

"Don't you need it?"

"Not here. It just causes problems."

She frowned. "Oh. The billiard ball. Amber's party. I see. Yah. Problems." She fiddled with his curls. "Are there others like you?"

He nodded.

"You can't tell me who they are?"

He nodded again.

She pulled him into a hug. "I could live with your mystery."

"Are you sure?"

She turned to lean her back on his chest. "I'm not sure of anything, remember? Except this. You and me. Doing whatever we set out to do. Together."

Florian held Kate like that for a while, in silence. Just listening to their breathing, their hearts beat in unison. Maybe they could make this unique relationship work.

The unfamiliar ring sounded again. Kate sat up. "That's weird."

"What is?"

"That's my iPad. The Skype ring." She stood, headed to the end of the kitchen counter, and slipped her tablet from her bag. She set it up on the stand and clicked the screen.

"Hello dear Kate Rose Delore," came an all-to-familiar voice. "How are you?"

Florian groaned. "Oh no."

"Uh, hello. I'm fine. Are you calling for Florian?" Kate turned to Florian. "Do you know him?" Then quieter she said, "Do I know him? He seems so familiar, so friendly. Like family. And how does he know my middle name?" She said that last bit softly, as if to herself, and stared at Florian without looking at him, trying to work it out.

"Kate, no, I'm calling for you, primarily." Uncle laughed good-naturedly.

"Uh, okay." Kate turned back to the screen. "Um, hi."

"You're looking well, Kate Rose."

Even Florian, despite his chagrin at being tracked down, couldn't help but smile at the warmth in Uncle's voice. He got up to stand beside Kate and tucked his arm around her waist, pulling her close.

"Thanks. Just Kate please. I am well." Kate glanced at Florian, and then at the screen again. "How can I help you, sir? And how do you know my full name?" She turned to Florian and whispered, "How does he know my middle name? I haven't even told you."

"Do you know who I am, Kate?" Uncle's round face filled the screen, his curly white hair and beard framing his red cheeks.

She shook her head. "Family? But I don't remember meeting you."

Uncle smiled kindly. "I'm Santa. And Florian is one of my nephews, and my newest Master Baker."

Florian sucked in his breath. "Uncle! The rules."

"I make the rules, son. Now let me talk to your girl."

Florian nodded, stunned.

"Santa! You do look like him," Kate said and shook her head.

"You don't seem surprised, dear."

Kate shrugged and smiled, squeezing Florian against her. "So my Florian is a Christmas Elf."

Santa smiled. "Indeed, and one of the best bakers I have ever had the pleasure to raise and eat with."

"Why?" Kate glanced at Florian, and then back to Uncle. "I don't really understand..."

"I want there to be more magic in the world, so this next generation is teaching me that magic needs to live in the Human world as much as at the Poles." There was some noise in the background. Uncle turned his head, and Florian caught a glimpse of the Master Office. His father looked up and winked at him.

Florian sucked in a breath. His father was in on this, whatever this was.

"Uncle?"

"Just a moment, nephew," Santa said, turning back to them. "Kate, do you understand?"

"No, not really."

"Florian is on loan to you, indefinitely. Make your wonderful cupcakes together and bring more magic and love into the world to children of all ages. I give you my blessing."

"Thank you. Santa." Kate wiped the tears from her eyes. "I promise—"

"No." Uncle raised a finger. "Promise only to each other. I only want you to send a box of cupcakes up here every year, for us and all the crew. For Christmas. First order in—" Uncle looked at his wristwatch that told the time in every time zone and included the date. "Fifteen days from your zone."

"I—we can do that, right?" Kate looked at him.

"Yah, sure. Of course, sir," Florian said, his head and heart reeling. "May I speak?"

"Just a moment, nephew. I'd like a word in private with your girl, if you don't mind," Uncle said.

Kate looked at him and shrugged. "I'll take it into the bedroom."

Florian nodded, and Kate walked into her bedroom carrying her tablet and shut the door.

Florian didn't know what to do with himself. The kitchen was neat and clean. The living room too. He pulled another wine glass out of the cupboard and set it beside the one Kate had set there earlier. Should he pour the wine now or wait until—?

Kate came out of the bedroom without the tablet, a teary smile on her face. "He wants to talk to you." She shook her head. "That's really Santa, isn't it?"

He kissed her.

She smiled broader and reached for him. He danced out of her reach.

"Yes, it is. Uncle to me. And I better not keep him waiting."

She nodded and stroked his cheek. It tickled his day-old beard. He hadn't shaved today. And he knew Kate liked it. He gave her a short kiss and headed for the bedroom. The tablet was on the nightstand. Florian sat on the edge of the bed and lifted up the iPad, the better to hear and see what Uncle had to say to him.

"Uncle? Hi."

Uncle smiled at him. "You have yourself a good one there, my lad. Treat her well."

"Yes sir."

"About your wild magic."

"It is a problem, I know. Unruly. Wayward. Mischievous." Florian frowned and waited to see if Uncle would add any more words, but he didn't so Florian barreled ahead. "I was just so jealous—"

"Fear and Anger are dangerous too, unless you transform them into courage and passion. Can you do that, young man?"

Florian nodded.

"Jealousy, too, you must transform that as well."

"Into what, Uncle?"

"Compassion and action toward what you love. And trust. And telling the truth."

Florian nodded. Courage, passion, compassion, action, trust, and telling the truth. Sounded like a motto. He could do that. "Uncle, you—you—why are you doing this?"

"I told you. With your gifts together, you and Kate can bring more love and magic into the world on a daily basis than I can do alone once a year."

"Like Christmas every day," Florian said softly.

"Yes, like that." Santa smiled broadly.

"You're breaking the rules for us."

Santa waved a wand. "And for your sister, Dahlia. And for Holly."

"Aunt Holly? How so?"

"That's her story to tell."

"Why?" Florian asked again.

Santa knew what he meant.

"Changes are afoot, and this is my way of helping to balance the scales."

Florian considered. "So we're pawns in a greater game."

"I need you and your sister and the others to bring the love and magic to the front lines. Not always behind the scenes. The time has come. The world is ready," Santa said.

"I trust you, Santa," Florian said. "Thank you."

"You better, my boy. Make us proud. Now there's someone here who would like to speak to you."

Santa stepped out of the frame.

"Mom! Dad!" Video calls were amazing.

Chapter Eighteen

"The passion we bring into the world with our gifts is a blessing. Share your gifts. Share your passion. You are the blessing."

Kate fiddled with the paper where she'd scrawled Santa's words to her. She sat on a stool at her tall kitchen counter, waiting for Florian to return from her bedroom and his chat with his uncle. Santa! Who would have thunk? She smiled and shook her head. No way. Yet, Florian being a Christmas elf added up—all those strange magical occurrences and his good nature and being a fast learner and who knew what else was special about him? It explained a lot of things.

She wanted to embrace him and jump up and down. What it meant for the future, she didn't know, except that she felt stronger now that she wasn't trying to do everything herself—she knew she could leap higher, risk more, love harder. She wiped the tears from the edge of her eyes and hopped off the stool. Time to unwrap Florian's lunch and celebrate.

In a few minutes, Florian came out of her bedroom with her tablet. He handed it to her and smiled. She smiled back and took the tablet. It was powered off.

He opened his arms and enveloped her in a hug. "Oh, Kate! I had no idea he would call. Or could call."

Kate felt his heart beating against her chest and squeezed. She pulled back and slipped her tablet back into her bag.

"I'm—I'm reeling from it...Did it really happen?" She gazed up at him.

"Pinch me. I'm real." Florian held out his arm.

"I know you're real—"

She pinched him anyway. He squeaked and then danced out of her reach. "If I'm real, so is Santa." Florian unwrapped the sandwiches she'd set on the counter. He opened drawers and found her silverware.

She slipped back onto her stool and watched Florian find his way around her galley kitchen. She fiddled with the page where she'd written Santa's words to her.

"Wine?" Florian gestured with a bottle of chilled Sebastiani Chardonnay.

"That'd be lovely." Kate blew out a breath to relieve some of the jumpy energy she felt in her solar plexus. "So...what did he say to you?"

Florian gazed at her with his sea-green eyes, full of warmth and something that made her heart speed up. He smiled and sniffed away what looked like coming tears. "He told me that with our gifts together, we can bring more love and magic into the world on a daily basis than he can do alone once a year."

"Like Christmas every day," Kate said, awed.

"That's what I said." Florian laughed and dished coleslaw on plates.

"Can we do that? Are we a team, Florian?" Kate asked.

"For as long as you'll have me, *grá*." He grinned. "That's Gaelic for love."

"I hoped it was." Kate took in the moment and smiled with joy, tears threatening to spill.

"I made lunch for us." Florian slide a plate to her, filled with one part coleslaw, one part a half sandwich, and one part a cupcake covered in chocolate frosting. The cupcake top was decorated with a Christmas tree outlined in green, ornamented with tiny red beads at the end of each tree branch.

"Florian!" She picked up the cupcake and admired it. "When did you make this? I love it."

He shrugged. "I was up early. Taste it."

"I love starting with dessert," she said and took a bite of the cupcake that tasted like orange and chocolate and a hint of something unexpected. "Lavender?" She licked her lips. "Hmmm. You have a winner here. What shall we call it?"

"Lavender Christmas," Florian said. "I made it for you. My gift to you."

She set the cupcake down on her plate. "You were ready to give up everything for me."

Florian nodded. "And you were willing to trust me and leap, even though I messed up and ruined the party and made a fool of myself in front of your customers, and your business is probably going to change into—"

"Into something new that I can't predict or control."

Kate's phone buzzed. She checked the screen. Alex's face popped up. The phone buzzed again.

"Are you going to answer that?" Florian asked. He took a bite of his sandwich and chewed, acting nonchalant and confident.

"I need to. To tell him myself what is going on with us." Kate slipped off the stool, kissed Florian on the lips, and headed toward the bedroom for privacy. "Hi Alex."

"How are you, Kate?" Alex's deep voice rumbled in his clipped British accent. "Did I catch you at a good time?"

On second thought, she needed to have this conversation out in the open. She headed back to the living room.

"Actually, I am busy."

"Well, this won't be long. I just wanted to let you know that I helped smooth things over with the Winthrop's. You know you can just ask me for help—"

"Thank you for that, Alex." She cleared her throat. "I'll handle the situation directly from now on."

"Can't a friend help?" Alex asked.

"Alex, I appreciate your help, but you're not my knight in shining armor. I'm sorry if I misled you in any way, but we're not getting back together." She felt Florian's gaze on her, but didn't turn to look.

"Oh, I—well, I didn't want to presume, but—Are you with that baker?"

"It's really none of your business, but yes."

"But you hardly know him," Alex said.

"Like I said, it's none of your business. I wish you the best, Alex, but please don't call me again," Kate said. She didn't wait, but disconnected the phone call.

She slipped the phone into her jean's pocket and said out loud, "I needed to do that a long time ago."

"So glad you did."

Beth Barany

Kate sat down again at the counter. "I didn't realize I left things hanging. But maybe it was the way I greeted him at Hank's party—"

"*Grá*, it's over." Florian tapped the note she'd written. "What's this?"

"Santa said it to me."

"It's true."

She smiled. "I know. I've been working so hard I lost sight of the bigger picture, of my purpose for doing this work. Why I decided to open my cupcake business here, instead of follow Alex to his next postdoc appointment to study mushrooms in Ancient Greek literature."

Florian laughed. "Really? That's what he studies."

"And he gets invited to foodie symposiums around the world."

"So a big wig."

"I guess. But I didn't want to be wingman, somebody's second. I want to run my own show, with a partner." Kate lifted her glass of wine. "With you. To us."

"To us." Florian lifted his glass. "And to passion, love, and—"

"Cupcakes." Kate clicked her glass against Florian's.

"Yes, to cupcakes!"

ACKNOWLEDGMENTS

Thank you so much to my early readers, critique partners, and brainstorming buddies: Beth Chapmon, Dodie Coe, Kimberley Anne Hoffman, Kay Keppler, Alex King, Lea Kirk, Cheryl Liquori, Carol Malone, Martin Reisberg, Suzanne Waligore. You all rock. The book is much better because of you, though any errors are entirely my own. Thank you also to my dear sweet husband. Let's cook up some more mischief!

ABOUT THE AUTHOR

Award-winning novelist Beth Barany writes magical tales of romance and adventure to enchant readers into worlds where anything is possible. In her off-hours, Beth enjoys gardening, walking, and watching movies with her husband, author Ezra Barany. Together they live in Oakland, California, with their cat and over 1,000 books.

You can sign up for Beth's newsletter for news and free books at her site: http://author.bethbarany.com, or follow her on Twitter and Facebook.

www.ingramcontent.com/pod-product-compliance
Lightning Source LLC
Chambersburg PA
CBHW051259250626
47155CB00009B/3351